Olivia's Enchanted Summer

Everything was working out fine for the Swans. They had three amazing weeks ahead of them, full of performing and adventure.

Olivia was suddenly distracted by her sister, Eel, who was pirouetting again, arms outstretched. "This is going to be the best summer ever!" she cried.

Olivia nodded. It was going to be glorious: an enchanted summer they'd never *ever* forget.

Have you read the other books in the series?

Olivia's First Term
Olivia Flies High
Olivia and the Movie Stars
Olivia's Winter Wonderland
Olivia and the Great Escape
Olivia's Curtain Call

"Hugely enjoyable"
The Stage

"Gripping"
Guardian

Olivia's
Enchanted Summer

LYN GARDNER

nosy
crow

First published in the UK in 2012 by Nosy Crow Ltd
The Crow's Nest, 10a Lant Street
London, SE1 1QR, UK

Nosy Crow and associated logos are trademarks and/or registered
trademarks of Nosy Crow Ltd

Text copyright © Lyn Gardner, 2012

The right of Lyn Gardner to be identified as the author of this work has
been asserted by her in accordance with the Copyright, Designs and
Patents Act 1988.

A CIP catalogue record for this book will be available from the
British Library.

All rights reserved

3 5 7 9 10 8 6 4

This book is sold subject to the condition that it shall not, by way of
trade or otherwise, be lent, hired out or otherwise circulated in any
form of binding or cover other than that in which it is published. No
part of this publication may be reproduced, stored in a retrieval system,
or transmitted in any form or by any means (electronic, mechanical,
photocopying, recording or otherwise) without the prior written
permission of Nosy Crow Ltd.

Printed and bound in the UK by Clays Ltd, St. Ives Plc
Typeset by Tiger Media Ltd, Bishops Stortford, Hertfordshire

Papers used by Nosy Crow are made from wood grown in
sustainable forests.

ISBN: 978 0 85763 048 3

www.nosycrow.com

Chapter One

Olivia Marvell stood by the railings at the top of the Mound and looked down over Edinburgh. Below her was a group of acrobats attempting a human pyramid and wobbling dangerously like a badly set jelly on a hot summer's day. Two teenage girls were doing a comic juggling act. One of them was juggling perfectly with what appeared to be half a dozen fresh eggs, but which Olivia suspected were rubber fakes. The other girl was throwing real eggs into the air and failing to catch them. They kept splatting on her partner's head, whose pretend anger was creating much hilarity among the crowd.

There was also a troupe of mad tap dancers wearing kilts who were doing an intricate routine to bagpipes and being cheered enthusiastically. Olivia smiled as she watched some small children trying to join in and falling over their own – and the dancers' – feet. She felt a mounting sense of excitement as if someone were hugging her insides very tightly.

It was a bright early August afternoon just a few days before the start of the Edinburgh Festival Fringe. A mass of people swirled below, all attracted to the Mound and its merry sights and sounds, and making Olivia think of the Pied Piper. It was as if the entire world was being drawn towards the city by an invisible thread of music and bright colours. She wished her friend, Tom, was here to see it, but he was playing John in a huge sell-out West End production of *Peter Pan* and wouldn't be free until the very end of August.

Olivia wheeled round as somebody touched her shoulder. It was Georgia and Aeysha.

"Hey!" she said, pleased to see her friends. "Did you get rid of all your posters?"

"All but one," said Aeysha, unfurling a midnight-blue A3 sheet dotted with silver stars. It showed a girl on a trapeze surrounded by fairies, and a magician and a sprite walking the high wire. Emblazoned across the top in small golden Gothic letters were the words: *The Swan Circus Presents*, and then in even bigger letters it read: *Enchantment: A Magical Circus Entertainment*. They had all looked at the poster many times before but it still made Olivia feel shivery with pleasure.

"Eel and I found people to take all of ours," she said. "Lots of shops are going to put them up in their windows. It helps that they're so striking. The woman in one of the cafés said she might even come and see our show after Eel did a crazy tap dance and stood on her head. I can't wait for the Swan Circus to appear in front of an audience!"

Olivia grinned at her friends and they grinned back. Aeysha winked and Georgia did a little skip. Olivia didn't have to say anything; she could tell from Georgia's doll-like face and Aeysha's sparkling eyes with their thick dark lashes that they felt as excited as she did.

Her little sister, Eel – so called because she could never stand still – was busy gyrating wildly to the beat of some distant drums. She had a real talent for dance. The two sisters had seen *Coppelia* performed by the Royal Ballet at the Royal Opera House in Covent Garden at the end of last term and Eel's mesmerising antics reminded Olivia of the life-sized dancing doll.

Eel had just done a spontaneous cartwheel and was starting to draw quite a crowd herself, obstructing the throng attempting to negotiate the steep steps up and down the Mound. Olivia always felt embarrassed when her little sister's dancing displays in public places attracted attention, so she grabbed her by the hand and started down the steps. Aeysha and Georgia followed.

Olivia hadn't gone far when there was a commotion and the sound of shouting behind her. Before she could turn round, she found herself being pushed roughly aside by a girl of about her own age, who was wearing a thin yellow cotton dress with a distinctive trim of blue cornflowers around the hem. She was racing down the stone steps two at a time as if she were being pursued by all the devils in hell. Her long plaits streamed behind her like two shiny black snakes, while Olivia couldn't help noticing that the backs of her legs were extremely grubby.

Olivia stumbled and lost her grip on Eel's hand, and she would have fallen if it wasn't for her own exceptional sense of balance, honed by many hours on the high-wire and trapeze, and because the quick-witted Aeysha caught her from behind with both hands and steadied her.

"Oi," shouted Olivia crossly. "Watch where you're going!"

Without breaking step, the girl in the yellow dress glanced round and for a fraction of a second her eyes met Olivia's. There was something about those eyes that reminded Olivia of a hunted deer and yet something defiant also glinted there. It felt as if the girl was daring Olivia to protest again.

Then the girl hurtled onwards, followed closely by a black-and-white Border collie. The collie dog whipped past Olivia but then suddenly turned back, sat down abruptly at Olivia's feet, raised a paw and gave a little yelp as if to say "Sorry". He then raced after the girl.

"Did you see that? That dog's amazing. It's almost as if he can talk. I'd swear he was trying to apologise," said Olivia, her eyes wide.

"He's got better manners than his mistress, then," said Georgia, watching as the girl in the yellow dress continued pell-mell down the steps, scattering people like skittles as she went. The collie bolted ahead of her, trying to herd the people out of the way as if they were sheep.

"I wonder why she's in such a mad rush?" said Aeysha thoughtfully. "It was almost like she was being chased."

"Maybe she's got a show to get to," replied Olivia.

"Well, *we've* got a show to put on," said Eel, "and it's going to be the best in Edinburgh." Unlike her older sister, Eel was always supremely confident. Olivia hoped that in this instance her little sister was right to be quite so optimistic.

The Edinburgh Festival was the biggest arts festival in the world, and Olivia, her friends and other pupils from their school, the Swan Academy of Theatre and Dance, were going to perform at the Fringe. They had been rehearsing hard long before school had broken up for the summer, and all the children taking part had had to sacrifice their family holidays, but they didn't mind. What was two weeks in Tenerife compared with appearing at the Edinburgh Fringe in the debut performance by the Swan Circus? It was too thrilling an opportunity to pass up; over the last sixty years many reputations had been made and lost in Edinburgh during the festival.

Lots of the Swans' families would be

coming up to Edinburgh for the final few days to see their children perform. Aeysha's big extended family were all coming, at least twenty of them, and Georgia's dad, who was separated from her mum, was bringing his new girlfriend, Leonie. Olivia and Eel didn't have any relatives to visit, but Olivia hoped that Tom would make it up to watch the last few performances.

At that very moment, Olivia's dad, Jack Marvell, the famous high-wire walker also known as the Great Marvello, and his friend Pablo, who taught circus skills at the Swan, were putting the finishing touches to the Swan Circus big top that had been erected on Calton Hill on the other side of Princes Street. Last night, they had turned on the lights on the outside of the big top for the first time, and Olivia, Eel, Georgia and Aeysha had gasped to see *Swan Circus* picked out in fairy lights and twinkling high above the great city. The craggy and forbidding castle perched on the other side of Edinburgh had seemed to be winking back at them. It had felt as if the whole city was bewitched.

Even in broad daylight, the scene below them was magical. It reminded Olivia of a medieval fair straight out of the pages of a history book. She could see and hear a band of Peruvian musicians, and a group of actors dressed in Elizabethan costume were wandering about just like a band of seventeenth-century strolling players. One of the actors was wearing a huge donkey's head and Olivia guessed that the troupe were performing *A Midsummer Night's Dream*.

She suddenly felt anxious. The Swan Circus performance also included a scene from *A Midsummer Night's Dream*, with the fairies played by children who had been taking Pablo's circus-skills course. Olivia knew it was good, innovative even, in the way it successfully melded circus, theatre and dance and even roller skating. But would anyone want to come and see their show when there were thousands to choose from? Some long-established theatre companies with serious reputations were at the Fringe this year. The National Theatre of Scotland was performing at the Pleasance, the Globe Theatre were taking their touring production of *Pericles* to the grounds of a local stately home, and Theo Deacon, a former Swan pupil and now a major Hollywood star, was in a controversial new play at the famous Traverse Theatre. The former soap star, Cassie Usher, who had played Maria in the production of *The Sound of Music* in which Georgia, Tom and Eel had also appeared, was performing her one-woman musical show in an inflatable upside-down purple cow in Bristo Square.

When Olivia had first seen the Fringe programme, she'd felt excited to be part of such a big festival, with so many people performing in so many places all over the city, not just in proper theatres. There was a show taking place in a telephone box on Grassmarket; one that took the form of a city-wide theatrical treasure hunt, and another on and around the swings in a children's playground. But then she had felt intimidated. Would anyone be prepared to make the trek up Calton Hill to see an unknown theatre-circus performance by a bunch of kids when there were so many other brilliant shows on at exactly the same time and in more central locations and at famous venues? If no one came, it would mean financial disaster for the Swan Circus and particularly for her dad, Jack, who had put everything he had into the venture.

Olivia had overheard her grandmother, Alicia, who also ran the Swan Academy, saying that Jack ought to put his name on the publicity because it would help draw a crowd and get them some media coverage. Jack had been insistent that their trip to the Edinburgh Fringe wasn't about him but about the Swans. Olivia thought that was just like her dad, who was generous to a fault. But it also demonstrated his lack of what her gran called "savvy" and others called common sense. She thought that Alicia was right, and Jack was silly not to use his fame to help sell some tickets. But he had stood firm, so his name wasn't even on the posters.

The Swan Circus was Jack's way of saying thank you to Alicia for taking the girls in and giving them a home and an education at her stage school after an accident had stopped him working. They had lost their travelling circus, and been left almost completely destitute. Olivia, who at first had been resentful of finding herself at a stage school, now loved learning to act and having such good friends as Georgia, Aeysha and Tom.

She wished Tom was here now to calm her nerves. Olivia missed him; it felt as if there was a huge Tom-shaped hole in her life and also in the show itself. She and Tom both had a natural gift for the high-wire. When Olivia had first arrived at the Swan and unhappiness had made her prickly and difficult, Tom had been the only person to believe in and stand by her. She missed being able to confide in him. Just then, as though he'd known what she was thinking, Olivia's phone bleeped with a message. *Just getting ready to fly in this afternoon's matinee. Hope Edinburgh and high-wire going fine. Tom x*

Olivia immediately texted back. *Edinburgh fab. High-wire with dad such fun. But miss u up there with me. Need u around, ready to catch me if i fall. Liv x*

Olivia's phone bleeped again almost as soon as she had pressed send. Tom had replied. *Liv Marvell never falls!*

Olivia grinned. She wished it was true. All high-wire walkers fell on occasion, even the very best like her dad.

"Come on, let's go and see what's going on down there," she said to the others. "We've still got almost half an hour before we need to meet Alicia and the others at Waverley Station."

Her friends nodded enthusiastically. Olivia grabbed Eel's hand again and they ran down the rest of the steps past some strange silvery statues. As they were passing one of the statues, it put out an arm and tapped Olivia on the shoulder, making her jump with shock and then double up with laughter. The statues weren't made of stone or metal but were performers standing very, very still. Olivia and the others gathered around the one who'd moved, a young woman dressed as the Snow Queen, and peered at her closely. She didn't even blink.

"I'd die if I had to stand still like that for hours," said Eel.

"You'd die if you had to stand still for a second," said Olivia. "Even in your sleep you're constantly wriggling. My legs are bruised all over."

For the last few nights they'd all been staying in a twin room in a cheap bed and breakfast, with Olivia and Eel sharing one bed and Georgia and Aeysha the other. But with the arrival of the rest of the Swans today they were all due to move into the big rented house that Jack had found for them on the Internet. They couldn't wait to see what it was like. It had been such a lucky find. The first house Jack had arranged to rent had fallen through the week before they were due to arrive in Edinburgh, so being able to find something else at the last moment had felt like a miracle. Jack's anxiety about it all had turned to triumph. Everything was working out fine. They had three amazing weeks ahead of them, full of performing and adventure.

Olivia was suddenly distracted by Eel, who was pirouetting again, arms outstretched. "This is going to be the best summer ever!" she cried.

Olivia nodded. It was going to be glorious: an enchanted summer they'd never *ever* forget.

Chapter Two

The girls wandered around, breathing in all the sights and smells and sounds. There were stalls selling everything from doughnuts to jewellery, set up among the pavement artists and caricaturists. But it was the performers who interested Olivia and the others most. Eel watched the tap dancers with a critical eye and decided that the kilts were a mistake, and that the Swans could dance better. She also decided that the bagpipes sounded like a cat in pain.

"I think bagpipes sound beautiful," said Georgia. "Like a mermaid weeping."

Aeysha grinned. "And when did you last hear a mermaid crying, Georgie?" she asked.

A great roar went up from the crowd as four fire-eaters juggled their flaming sticks and then gobbled up the flames as if they were candyfloss. Olivia's attention was caught by a flash of yellow in the corner of her eye. She turned and there, a few metres away, was the girl in the yellow dress. She was talking urgently to a beautiful girl of about sixteen or seventeen. The older girl was crying, and the Border collie nuzzled her legs as if trying to comfort her. Olivia was certain that the two were sisters. They had the same thick, glossy, black hair. The girl in the yellow dress kept looking anxiously around as if expecting trouble at any minute, and she was clearly trying to persuade the older girl to leave.

Suddenly, she tugged at her arm and nodded up the steps. Olivia glimpsed a thickset man pushing his way down the Mound steps, knocking aside anyone who got in his way. The Border collie ran to the steps and bounded up them at top speed. The man aimed a kick at the dog but lost his balance. He teetered on the edge of the steps before falling to the ground, like a large tree whose trunk had been axed, and was immediately surrounded by concerned passers-by.

The dog bounded back down the steps. Olivia turned to look for the sisters again. They had vanished into thin air. It was as if the dog had deliberately tripped the man up so they could get away. She wondered briefly why he was following them before being distracted by a crowd gathering at the back of the National Gallery of Scotland. She couldn't see what they were looking at but she wanted to know what it was. The fire-eaters were reaching the end of their act so Olivia beckoned to the others to follow her. They still had ten minutes before they had to go to the station to meet the rest of the Swans off the London train. The girls worked their way through the crowd and stopped when they got the near the front.

A small boy, aged about ten, with light brown hair and eyes that crinkled when he smiled, was walking around the circle of people. He wore a black cloak over his shoulders that glittered with stars and crescent moons, and a top hat that was rather too big for him which he had to keep pushing up above his eyes. It was slightly comical and very endearing, but the boy seemed oblivious to his own charm and his face was serious.

Talking continuously, the boy walked slowly around the circle, then stopped in front of a woman, reached up behind her right ear and produced an egg still in its shell. Then with a flourish he reached behind her left ear and produced another egg – but this one was fried. The woman blushed, and the crowd giggled and gasped. The boy continued around the circle, stopping every now and again in front of someone. A bored-looking man who kept glancing impatiently at his watch suddenly burst into laughter when the boy pulled what seemed to be a never-ending chain of watches from his shirt pocket, and a pretty teenager turned quite pink when the boy lifted up her straw hat to reveal a tomato perched on her head.

Everyone clapped and cheered. The boy continued around the circle and then stopped in front of Eel, whose chestnut curls were in complete disarray.

"Bird's-nest hair," he said with a cheeky grin. Eel looked comically affronted, but her expression turned to wonder as the boy leaned forward, put his hands behind her head and produced a cooing dove whose ruffled breast had an iridescent mother of pearl sheen. Olivia and the others gasped out loud. The boy put the dove in a gilded cage that was sitting on a small table covered with a red velvet tablecloth. He put a black cloth over the ornate domed cage, passed his hands over the top, then removed the black cloth. There, sitting in the cage in the spot where the dove had been, was a silver-grey dwarf rabbit with the same pinky glow on its fur as the dove's breast.

The crowd erupted. Olivia and the others stared at each other open-mouthed. It was impossible. They couldn't believe their own eyes. How had he made the switch without them noticing?

Suddenly, there was a commotion to the right of the circle and Olivia saw that the girl in the yellow dress had barged her way to the front, much to the annoyance of those she'd shoved aside. The small magician moved around the circle and stopped close to the girl. He leaned forward and produced a marble from each of her ears. The girl looked unimpressed. Then he asked with a grin, "Are you sure you haven't lost something?"

The girl shook her head with a jaunty confidence, before hesitating and feeling in one pocket and then another. The boy watched her with a look of friendly amusement, but the panicked girl's face contorted with rage as her search failed to yield the thing she was looking for.

"Give it back!" she shouted in an accent that was Scottish but with just a trace of something more exotic. "Give it back, you nasty little pickpocket!"

Unfazed and still smiling, the boy held up a sapphire necklace that caught the bright sunlight and sparkled as if it was dancing. The crowd *oohed*, and a small child asked, "Is it real?"

"Of course not, it's just pretend," said her mum, smiling.

"It looks real," said Eel.

The girl was certainly behaving as if it was real. "You're a thief," she shouted at the boy, her dark eyes blazing. Her voice rose to a screech. "He sent you to steal it back, didn't he? You're a sneaky thief."

Confusion crossed the boy's face. He suddenly looked uncertain and vulnerable, and Olivia felt sorry for him. She'd seen enough magicians when she'd been with the travelling circus to know that he wasn't a thief. Filching the necklace without the girl knowing had just been part of his magic act, done to amaze the audience and make them whoop and clap.

"No, he's not," she said sharply to the girl. "It's just a trick. He's not going to keep it."

The boy smiled gratefully at Olivia and nodded vigorously, but the girl glared at her as if she wanted to kill her.

"Who do you think you are to interfere?" she snapped. "Keep your stuck-up nose out of it."

"Evie…"said her older sister warningly as she appeared at her side.

"You're the one being rude, and you seem to make a habit of it," replied Olivia hotly. She felt Georgia's calming hand on her sleeve. The girl's fists clenched and her eyes sparkled dangerously.

"Please," said the boy quietly, "I didn't mean to upset you. Take your necklace and look after it well if it's so precious to you." He held it out to the angry girl. She snatched it from his hand and pushed her way out of the circle.

She was followed by her sister, who had turned scarlet with embarrassment. Olivia heard her mutter, "I thought we were trying to keep a low profile, Evie," as they passed. The crowd tutted at them, and the boy looked crushed. He knew that the mood was fatally broken; the act ruined.

"Show over," he said quietly and began to pack up his things. The crowd drifted away towards a young ventriloquist whose dummy was dressed like a naughty schoolboy. Aeysha pulled at Olivia's sleeve and pointed at her watch. They had about five minutes to get to Waverley Station to meet the London train.

Olivia felt reluctant to hurry away. She felt sorry for the boy and she was fascinated by his skill. But there was something more. She had an uncanny feeling that she knew him from somewhere. She wondered what show the boy was appearing in at the Fringe. Instead of following the others, she stepped towards him.

"You were amazing," she said shyly. The boy grinned. There was something about his manner, and in particular his grin, that was really very familiar.

"So were you; you were brave to say what you did to that girl," said the boy and he leaned forward and plucked a ruby earring from each of her ears.

"How do you do that?" asked Olivia wonderingly.

The boy put a finger to his lips. "It's my secret," he said. "But things are not always what they appear. You can't always trust your eyes."

They both jumped as a shout came from a few metres away. "LIVY!" bawled Eel at the top of her lungs.

"We're going to be late!" yelled Georgia.

"I've got to go," said Olivia apologetically and she ran to catch up with the others. She suddenly realised that she had forgotten to ask the boy his name or which show he was in, but she didn't have time to go back now. She would have to comb through the Fringe brochure and see if she could spot a likely show.

The girls ran down into the station just as the London train pulled in.

"Phew, lucky it's a bit late," said Aeysha.

"That magician was totally ace," said Georgia, "even if that girl was incredibly rude."

"He was mega," said Eel. "I wish he could be in our show. He'd fit in so well, and be a real draw. We could do with some real magic in a show called *Enchantment*. Maybe we should tell Jack and Gran about him?"

"But he's not a Swan," said Aeysha.

"I'm not sure that would matter," said

Olivia. "And Eel's right, a show about magic ought to have some in it."

"I just meant it seems odd to have somebody we don't know and who isn't connected with the Swan in the Swan Circus," said Aeysha.

"Yes," said Georgia. "Being a Swan is like being part of a real family." She said it quite fiercely. Eighteen months ago, Georgia's dad had left her mum and, although she loved her mum, she missed her dad and still hadn't got used to being a family of two rather than three. Aeysha recognised something wistful in Georgia's voice and smiled sympathetically at her friend, but Olivia wasn't really listening. She was trying to think who it was the boy had reminded her of. It wasn't so much how he looked but the way he moved, his mannerisms and his smile.

People were starting to get off the train and walk up the platform.

"Come on, Livy. I can see Gran and Kylie and Will," said Eel. "And there's your mum, Georgia!"

Eel started waving madly and almost knocked over a placard for the *Edinburgh Evening News*. Olivia was struck by the headline: *Serial Jewel Thief Foiled. Police now have fingerprint lead*. She thought it sounded like an Enid Blyton novel.

Olivia watched as Eel shook her chestnut curls like a dog, before running towards her friends and flinging herself into her grandmother's arms, grinning broadly. In that instant Olivia realised who the boy reminded her of: Eel. And if he looked like Eel then he looked like Jack, too. Everybody always said how similar Eel and Jack were, whereas Olivia took after her mother, Toni. She remembered seeing a photograph of Jack that had been taken when he was about ten. Maybe her mind was playing tricks on her, but she'd swear that Jack and the boy were like two peas in a pod. She suddenly felt very strange and she didn't hear her dad come up and touch her on the shoulder.

"Can you hurry everyone up, Liv? Pablo's parked the bus on a yellow line and is fending off traffic wardens with charm and a pretend lack of English. We can't afford to get a parking ticket."

Olivia turned towards her father.

"Are you all right, chick?" he asked, seeing how pensive she was. "You look as if you've seen a ghost."

"I'm fine," insisted Olivia. She peered at her dad. He looked pale and vulnerable, as if he hadn't slept well. She suddenly remembered the date. If her mum hadn't died in a plane crash when Olivia was five and Eel just a baby, it would have been her birthday today. In all the excitement of being in Edinburgh, she had completely forgotten. She knew that Jack wouldn't want her to make a big deal out of it, but she also knew that he still missed Toni more than he could say. She reached for his hand and squeezed it.

"You're the best dad in the whole world," she said, "and I love you loads."

Chapter Three

"It must be around here somewhere," said Jack. His voice was tight with frustration.

"Maybe you're not reading the map right, Dad," said Eel helpfully. "Shall I do it? I'm very good at map-reading."

"I think your father knows how to read a map, Eel," said Alicia. "He managed to navigate his way out of the Idaho wilderness without your help," she added. What she didn't say was that the days after his light aircraft had crashed and he'd been missing, presumed dead, had been some of the worst of their lives.

Alicia sat behind Pablo, who was driving the old bus that Jack had hired for the summer. Dressed in her trademark dark-green velvet skirt, Alicia still looked as crisp as an apple even after the long journey from London to Edinburgh and even though she was suffering badly from the arthritis that had prematurely ended her stage career.

Everybody else looked wrecked. William Todd had spilled cranberry juice all down his shirt and looked as if he had had a sticky encounter with a vampire; Kylie had eaten so much chocolate on the train that she now felt both sick and homesick. Emmy Lovedale had just discovered that she had left her beloved teddy bear, Mr Bossyboots, on the train and began to wail. Georgia's mum, Lydia, who was there as chaperone, tried to soothe her by saying she would call Lost Property as soon as they had settled into the house. The huge pile of rucksacks and sleeping bags on the floor of the bus made them look like a group of refugees.

Not that anyone minded. Alicia, or Miss Swan as the children called her, liked the Swans always to look neat and professional, but although the children would be representing the school in Edinburgh they were also on their summer holidays and Alicia knew that they needed to relax. During term-time the Swans' lives were highly pressured: not only did they have to do all their school work and take the public exams that all children took, but they also took part in daily vocational classes, including acting, dancing and singing, and often worked professionally too, both in the West End and in movies and on TV.

The rest of the Swans began the final part of their journey in high spirits. Jack and Pablo took everyone up Calton Hill and they were all hugely impressed by the big top. They met up with Kasha and his band, who would be providing live music for the show as well as helping Pablo and Jack with the rigging. Kasha, who was sixteen, had just left the Swan. He'd already signed to a record label and would start work on his first album in the autumn. He and his friends, Ryan and Jazz, had been in Edinburgh for a couple of days helping Jack and Pablo erect the tent. They were sleeping in the living room of Kasha's aunt's little flat in the New Town.

Next, Jack suggested that the Swans go and settle into the rented house, have a bowl of pasta and all gather later at the tent for the technical rehearsal.

The children piled back on to the bus, laughing and jostling. Georgia and Will led a riotous singalong of "We're all going on a summer holiday". They squealed when they spotted a poster for their own show in a sweet-shop window, making Alicia put her hands over her ears, saying that they sounded like overexcited piglets.

"It just looks so lovely," said Kylie dreamily, who had quickly forgotten about feeling sick.

"I'd go and see us," said Eel.

"Let's hope other people feel the same," said Alicia. "We need to sell lots of tickets. It's a big risk doing a show at the Fringe, so many companies lose a great deal of money."

Soon they found themselves stuck in traffic on the Lothian Road just outside one of the big hotels.

Georgia nudged Olivia. "Look, it's that collie dog again. I wonder where his mistress is." The dog was sitting patiently down a side passage near the front of the hotel.

"Maybe she's in the hotel?" said Olivia. "Anyway, how do you know it's the same dog? One collie looks much like another to me."

"From the markings, silly," said Georgia, who had a very lively Jack Russell at home and knew about dogs.

"I wonder what she's doing in a grand hotel like that," said Olivia curiously.

The bus inched forward and as it did, the girl in the yellow dress and her sister came flying out of the hotel and into the road, dodging the traffic, followed by the dog. The younger girl barged into a man carrying a can of drink, which spilled all over her, but she didn't break stride, simply disappeared with her sister and the dog down a street by a clock tower.

Everyone on the bus was tired and hungry, and couldn't wait to get to the house, but Jack accidentally directed Pablo into a maze of back streets, where they got hopelessly lost for quite a long time. The map Jack had been sent by the landlord was lacking in detail. Then to everyone's relief, after several false turns and getting out to ask directions, they found Jekyll Street at last.

"Right," said Jack. "Everyone look out for number 13."

"Unlucky for some," said Aeysha.

"Not for us," said Eel confidently. "I've seen the photos of the house online. And done a virtual tour. I've even chosen my bedroom. Well, the one I'm going to share with four of you lot. It looks mint."

They drove slowly down the street, looking at all the numbers on the doors. The houses in Jekyll Street were large but mostly run-down and many were divided into flats and bedsits with several bells on the side of peeling front doors. Most of the front gardens were unkempt, and some were littered with rubbish, broken bicycles and old fridges. The windows were grimy and hung with net curtains more grey than white.

Alicia shifted uncomfortably in her seat. She wasn't sure this was quite what the Swans' parents would have envisaged from the letter she'd sent home with pupils, with its description of the prospective accommodation as "secure, spacious and in a good part of the city close to the centre".

"We must be very close," said Olivia, pointing to number 29. The children started counting down the numbers of the houses as they passed them.

"27...25...23...21..." Everyone shouted louder as they got closer. "...19...17...15..." Then there was a stunned silence. There was no number 13. The house numbers jumped from

15 to number 11. In the space where number 13 should have been was a short grit drive with grass growing up the middle leading down to some old garages.

Pablo stopped the bus, and Jack leapt out. "I'm going to take a look down there," he said, pointing at the drive that led between two dark houses. "Number 13 must be somewhere out the back behind one of the other houses."

Most people got out and followed him. They couldn't wait to see where they would be staying. But when they got to the end of the driveway, there was nothing but a row of six garages with battered, padlocked doors. The garage at the end of the row had a small dirty window high up in its pebble-dashed walls. Olivia noticed that someone had placed a small vase of fresh wild flowers on the inside sill. How odd. Who put flowers inside a garage?

"This isn't right. We must be in the wrong place," said Georgia.

"But this is definitely Jekyll Street," said Aeysha.

"Dad, you must have got the house number wrong," said Eel.

Jack shook his head. His face was tense.

Pablo came to join them and the two men talked together in low tones. Jack felt for his phone and punched in a number. Olivia could see that he was clenching the phone so hard that his knuckles had gone white. He waited for a moment, his face expectant.

"The number's not recognised. It says please check and try again," he said, running his hand distractedly through his hair. "I must have misdialled. I'm sure it's all going to be fine. I only spoke to the owner, Mitch, yesterday when I arranged the final money transfer."

The words "money transfer" hung in the air ominously. The children looked at each other, and Alicia pursed her lips. There was a steely glint in her eye. She had always thought that her son-in-law veered towards the reckless and irresponsible. Since Olivia and Eel had come to live with her at the Swan Academy, Jack and Alicia had begun to get to know each other better and their relationship had become increasingly warm. But they were like chalk and cheese – Alicia was organised, careful and cautious, while Jack was impetuous, romantic and worked almost entirely on instinct.

"Listen," said Jack. "Let's get back on the

bus and I'll e-mail Mitch. I'm sure it's just a silly mix-up."

They all piled back on to the bus, and Jack got out his laptop and sent an e-mail. Everyone was so quiet that the almost instant ping of the e-mail being boomeranged back was clear for all to hear, and those looking over Jack's shoulder could see that the message had been returned to sender.

Jack gave a low sigh. He'd always intended to come and check out the house before he paid over the bulk of the money, but once they'd arrived in Edinburgh he'd been so busy setting up the big top, it just hadn't seemed like a priority. In any case, the man had seemed so friendly in e-mails and on the phone. He'd even said how pleased he was to be renting to a circus troupe because he had family connections with the circus and loved it so much.

"Will we have to go back to London?" asked Eel, with a quiver in her voice.

"No," said Jack. "It's all going to be all right. I promise." But he knew that he had been foolishly naive and was increasingly certain he had fallen victim to an Internet scam.

"I'm sure it will all be fine," said Alicia. But

her voice was tight. "I'm confident Jack made all the necessary checks to make sure that the deal was bona fide."

Olivia felt furious with her. Pablo turned on the engine as if suddenly eager to be away from Jekyll Road.

"Wait," said Jack. "I'm just going to take one more look." He opened the door and started walking, alone, down the drive.

The tension in the bus was so high it felt to Olivia as if you could reach out with your hand and snap the air in two. Everyone was watching Jack's hunched back as if willing him to suddenly turn back and say that number 13 was there after all and they had just failed to notice it. To Olivia, her dad looked like the loneliest man in the entire world. She scrambled out of the bus and ran after him, before taking his hand and squeezing it tight.

They reached the garages. Jack looked around as if hoping for some kind of miracle and that a large, seven-bedroom, three-bathroom house with two reception rooms and a modern kitchen would suddenly appear from nowhere like magic. He buried his face in his hands.

"I've fouled up, big time, Liv," he said.

"It seemed such a good deal, but I was naive and I let myself be scammed. When I spoke to Mitch he sounded so plausible. There were even pictures of the house. I'm such a fool. I'm not a kid – by my age I should have learned that you can't believe everything you see and when something looks too good to be true, it probably is. Mitch just seemed so nice on the phone and in his e-mails. I'm such an idiot."

Olivia put her arms around his waist and gave him a hug. "You're not an idiot," she said. "You're the bravest and best dad in the world. Maybe you're just not the greatest at business, but it'll all work out OK in the end."

But she didn't really see how it could. Where would they stay? How would they pay for it? She wondered if Eel was right and they would have to abandon their show and return to London. She had always trusted her father so completely, had always believed that if there was a problem, he'd be able to solve it. He was her dad, wasn't he? He knew how to make things right. But she wasn't sure he could make things right this time.

"You need to report what's happened to the police," she said, and even as she said it, she felt as if she were the sensible grown-up and Jack the bewildered child.

Jack nodded. "I'd rather like to find this Mitch myself," he said, "but I don't know where to start and besides it's probably not a good idea. Come on, chick, let's go and join the others and work out what to do."

Olivia turned reluctantly, and she noticed the vase of flowers again. It made her curious. Jack had already started trudging down the path. She jumped on to the drainpipe that ran down the side of the building, then shimmied up until she was at eye level with the dirty little window near the roof of the garage. Olivia moistened her thumb with saliva, used it to wipe away the grime and peered in.

The garage was gloomy and she couldn't see much except piles of boxes and crates. But then she noticed some camp beds and bedding on the floor, a tiny little gas stove and saucepan, and two tins of beans. It looked as if someone was camping out in the garage. There was a dog bowl filled with water in the corner.

Olivia twisted her head to get a better look at one of the beds. It was covered by a blue sleeping bag, and just peeping out from underneath was a yellow dress with a distinctive blue trim. Olivia slithered down the pipe in surprise. The rude girl in the yellow dress must be living here with her sister and the collie dog! It was such an amazing coincidence. She couldn't wait to tell Georgia and Aeysha.

As she and Jack arrived back at the bus, an elderly woman walked by, dragging a small yapping poodle behind her.

"Excuse me," said Jack. "You don't happen to know if there's a number 13 Jekyll Road?"

The woman looked surprised. "Goodness no, not for years. It burned down ages ago, when I was still quite young. It was a terrible tragedy." The woman was clearly lonely and pleased to get the chance to chat. She talked on and on while Jack and Olivia nodded politely, although Olivia could tell her dad was eager to get away. Finally the woman concluded: "The house was never rebuilt. Lots of people are superstitious and don't want to live in a house with an unlucky number or on a plot with a bad history."

They thanked the woman and got back on to the bus. Everyone could tell from their faces that there was no hope.

"So," said Pablo, "what do we do now?"

"We go back to Calton Hill and consider our options," said Jack.

"I'm not sure we've got any options," said Alicia quietly but with such intensity that Olivia knew as soon as Alicia got Jack alone, she was going to give him an earful. She wouldn't like to be in her dad's shoes when that happened.

Chapter Four

Olivia walked along the tightrope, stumbled slightly and jumped off just before she lost her balance completely and fell. Normally, she loved walking the wire, and even if she was feeling down it always cheered her up, but her heart wasn't really in it today. What was the point of practising any part of her routine when she might never get to perform it? The day had curdled. The time on the Mound, the girl in the yellow dress and the boy-magician all seemed like a long-ago dream that had turned into a nightmare. She had spent some time poring over the Fringe programme in the hope of spotting the show the boy-magician might be in, but with no success.

Everyone's luggage was piled up in the

middle of the big top and the children were all sitting around, playing cards or reading. The sandwiches they had bought on the way back to Calton Hill lay half-eaten on the floor. Most people had lost their appetite and nobody could quite settle to anything. Eel, Aeysha and Georgia had tried to practise their excerpt from *Swan Lake*, which formed part of the show's witty, opening number, but like Olivia they couldn't concentrate and had given up.

Eel was now flicking through a book about famous ballerinas, and Georgia and Aeysha had just given up on a game of cheat with Will, Kylie and a Year Ten boy called Connor O'Toole, and come over to join Olivia. Everyone was very subdued. They knew that they might all be back on the train to London before the day was out unless they could find somewhere to stay. Olivia's phone bleeped with a message from Tom asking what the house was like.

Olivia sighed as she texted back: *House? What house? Turned out to be a figment of someone's imagination. That's the trouble with having a dad who believes everything he sees on the Internet. Disaster. Will explain all later.*

"What else did that woman say, Livy?"

asked Aeysha, who had been trying to quiz Olivia about the garages since they had arrived back at the big top.

"Oh, it was so sad," said Olivia. "When the house burned down there was a family living there, and the mum and dad were killed. There was a little girl who survived. But the woman didn't know what happened to her. She thought she was sent to stay with an aunt or something."

"How awful," said Georgia.

Olivia shook her head. "I know. She'd be pretty grown up by now, of course. At least as old as Dad." She paused, and added: "But I did see something interesting…"

"What?" asked Aeysha.

Olivia told them about looking through the garage window, and how she was certain that the girl in the yellow dress, her sister and the collie dog were living there.

"Why would they be living in a garage?" asked Georgia. "It must be really uncomfortable. Even though it's summer and warm and dry."

"I don't know," said Olivia.

"Maybe we should tell Miss Swan or your dad?" said Aeysha.

"I was going to tell Jack," said Olivia,

"but I thought he had enough to worry about. Anyway, if they want to live in a garage, it's their business. I don't care. We'll probably never see them again. At least they've got a roof over their heads, which is more than we do."

As soon as they'd got back to the big top, Jack had gone online and started trying to find an alternative place to stay. Alicia had rung the Fringe office and got a list of letting agencies and hotels, and she and Pablo and Georgia's mum, Lydia, had started to ring round. But it felt like every available house and flat in the city had already been let, and the bed-and-breakfasts and hotels were either full up or way too expensive. Jack was looking increasingly desperate.

"Well," said Alicia, flipping her phone shut. "That's the last place on the list. They can't help us, either. I know it's tough, Jack, but we're going to have to make some kind of decision. I've got a duty to the children's parents to keep them safe and that includes making sure that they've got somewhere to stay. Unless you've got a better idea, I think we have no choice but to return to London. Perhaps we'll be able to come back in a few days' time if you've managed to find some suitable accommodation."

Jack shook his head. He knew that if the Swans went back to London, they would never return and his dream of a Swan Circus would crumble to dust. He wasn't sure that his relationship with Alicia would survive such a disaster, either.

"Let's go outside and discuss it," he said.

Olivia hadn't meant to eavesdrop. She had simply gone to one of the portaloos that had been set up a little way away from the tent, close to where the bus was parked. Alicia and Jack were leaning against the bus talking and they didn't see Olivia enter the little green cubicle. But once she was inside she realised that she could hear them quite clearly and she couldn't resist listening.

"Well, that's that," said Alicia with a steely finality. "Either we go back to London, or you think again about my other suggestion. As far as I can see it's our only other option, but if you won't do it, Jack, I can't force you."

"I can't do it," said Jack. "Not after all these years. I saw Alfie's birth announced in a newspaper and that would have been the time to get in touch. He must be about ten now. I feel terrible that I've never even seen him, never sent word, never tried to heal the hurt, say I was sorry for what I did and admit I was responsible for such a huge betrayal."

"It caused a lot of pain," said Alicia, so quietly that Olivia could barely hear her.

"I know that," said Jack, sounding really upset. "It was the one thing that Toni and I never talked about, though we discussed everything else. We had no secrets from each other but that was the one thing that was out of bounds. It was too painful for both of us, and I felt too ashamed of what I'd done. And guilty."

"You can't change the past," said Alicia. "So maybe you could take this opportunity to put things right–"

Jack cut her off. "How could I possibly call up out of the blue and say: 'Hi, I just happen to be in Edinburgh and I know I haven't seen you for years and I did a terrible thing but I thought I might move in with you for the rest of month, and oh, I'm sure you won't mind at all, but I'll be bringing twenty children with me, including Toni's and my daughters.'"

"If you can't do it, I could," said Alicia quietly.

"Have you kept in touch all this time?"

demanded Jack hotly. "Did Toni know?" He didn't wait for an answer. "Don't meddle, Alicia. It was mine and Toni's business, not yours. What happened *happened*. I don't feel proud about how I behaved but I can't change anything now. It's too late."

"It's never too late with family. It wasn't too late for us, remember," said Alicia desperately.

Olivia opened the door of the portaloo and crept away. She felt like a thief who had stolen something that didn't belong to her. Secrets. But she could make neither head nor tail of it all. She was trembling slightly. What had her dad done that was so terrible, so awful that he hadn't even been able to discuss it with her mum and that he referred to as a betrayal? Everybody always said that her dad and mum's marriage had been a great love affair, just like in *Romeo and Juliet*. She remembered the Swan acting teacher, Sebastian Shaw, telling her about them during her first unhappy term at the school. He had said that it had been love at first sight but that their relationship had come at a cost. Olivia wasn't sure what he'd meant by that beyond the fact that it had temporarily estranged Toni from her mum. But what could Jack have possibly done that made him feel so ashamed, and who was this Alfie person?

Olivia's brain was all of a whirl. Whatever her father had done, he wasn't prepared to risk it being found out even to save the Swan Circus. She suddenly felt a surge of anger towards him. It was his fault that they were in this mess. He had mucked up. Everyone knew that you had to take care on the Internet. Things weren't always what they seemed. Even Eel knew that and she was only eight. Olivia had always felt so proud of her dad. People often called him a real-life latter-day hero for his amazing high-wire stunts such as walking across the Niagara Falls. To her he was just Jack, her dad, and he could do no wrong. But now he'd landed them in this mess *and* he had a dark secret, too. She felt the scratchy, itchy feeling in her throat that she knew meant tears. She swallowed hard and stomped back into the tent and sat down by herself a little way away from everyone else. Aeysha looked up, surprised, but just then, Jack, Alicia and Pablo appeared in the tent doorway. They looked serious.

"Gather round, everyone, " said Alicia. The children all moved towards them. Alicia looked at Jack. Jack cleared his throat. He looked really uncomfortable, his face chalky.

"We've explored every avenue, and I'm afraid it's bad news." A great groan went up from the children. "I'm sorry, we've no choice but to go back to London."

There were wails of disappointment and Eel wasn't the only one to burst out crying. Jack looked as if he might be close to tears, too.

"I'm so, so sorry," he said. "I've let you all down."

Eel ran towards him and gave him a hug, but Olivia didn't move. "Are you absolutely sure that you've explored every possibility?" she suddenly asked loudly. "Are you sure there isn't somebody you know who we can stay with, even just for a few days while we get sorted?"

Alicia glanced expectantly at Jack, and Jack stared at Olivia as if puzzled by the challenging edge in her voice.

"No, Liv, I'm sorry. There's nobody," he said, and he averted his gaze as if he couldn't bear her scrutiny. Olivia felt hot and angry. What was Jack hiding?

"Please gather your things," said Alicia. "If we hurry we might get the train that leaves in forty minutes. I'll ring all your parents, and of course anyone who needs to stay at the Swan will be able to; there's plenty of room, though the work on extending into the next-door building is a bit noisy."

Everyone began to collect their belongings in total silence.

"It's so sad our Edinburgh adventure has ended before it really began," said Aeysha. "Your dad looks really cut up about it."

Olivia shrugged, disappointment making her blood boil. "It's his own fault, he shouldn't have been so stupid. Everything's ruined because of him! Everyone thinks he's such a hero, and he is. But he's rubbish at all the practical stuff, and because he didn't sort it out properly we have to go back to London and the summer is totally spoilt."

Georgia and Aeysha looked at Olivia in surprise. She was normally Jack's greatest champion. Olivia ignored them as she packed her rucksack miserably. It had been a long and exhausting day. Now she'd never know which show the boy-magician was in. She began to roll up her sleeping bag and wondered again about the rude, prickly girl in the yellow dress and her sister. Why were they running from that man and why were they camping out in a garage? Camping out! She suddenly felt a surge of excitement like tiny pinpricks all over her skin.

"Wait, everyone, I've got an idea!"

Everyone turned to look at Olivia, their faces expectant.

"We could camp!" she cried, excitedly. "There must a campsite somewhere close to Edinburgh. Even if it's miles away, we could drive in each day. We've all brought sleeping bags. We'd just need to buy some cheap tents." Even before she'd finished speaking, a buzz of excitement had started to go round the group, Kylie and Connor were high-fiving each other and Jack had his laptop open as he feverishly searched the Web.

"That's a brilliant idea, Liv!" said Jack, entering "Edinburgh" and "campsites" into a search engine without looking up. "You're a genius." But Olivia didn't smile at his praise, and as she watched him there was a question in her eyes.

Chapter Five

Kasha and his band were playing a mesmerising piece of music that sounded like something a snakecharmer might use. It was strange and exotic, almost a little creepy in the way it curled around insistently inside your head like musical smoke.

Olivia, wearing a gauzy white costume shot through with silver thread so that she looked like a sprite, was hanging upside down on the trapeze and flying through the air as if possessed. Jack walked nimbly across the tightrope, turning and whirling; a staff helped him keep his balance. He was wearing a midnight-blue cloak covered in tiny silver stars and looked very dashing.

As in many of the scenes in the Swan Circus

show, Olivia and Jack were playing characters from Shakespeare, in this case the spirit Ariel and the magician Prospero from *The Tempest*. Below them in the ring, the Swan children were balancing on piles of old, leather-bound books that looked like ancient magical tomes, and building a human tower that rose higher and higher into the air.

The music reached a climax and Jack broke the staff in half as Prospero renounced his magic for ever. There was a shower of sparks as the staff broke and parchment and spells fell down on the auditorium like ancient faded confetti. The music ceased abruptly and there was a total blackout. Immediately Will Todd's cheeky face appeared in a circle of light and he launched into Puck's final speech from *A Midsummer Night's Dream*.

> "If we shadows have offended,
> Think but this, and all is mended,
> That you have but slumber'd here
> While these visions did appear."

Will continued through to the end of the speech and ended with a flourish.

"Give me your hands, if we be friends,
And Robin shall restore amends."

Kasha hit the triangle three times and then there was an eerie silence. From the front seats came the sound of four hands clapping. Lydia was shouting, "Bravo." Leaning on her stick, Alicia smiled as the lights came up. "I'm very proud of you all," she said. "It's a show that really lives up to its name, it is genuinely enchanting. You deserve to be a big success. Well done, Swans."

"Brilliant, everyone," said Jack. "Better a late dress rehearsal than no dress rehearsal. If you can do that well when we perform in front of an audience, we'll have a hit on our hands." He looked at his watch. "There's just over two hours before you make your Edinburgh debuts, so take off your costumes, hang them up, stretch, relax a little and have something to eat if you want. But nothing heavy. Everybody needs to be back here in one hour in costume and ready to warm up again."

The reason they were having such a late dress rehearsal was because they'd spent the afternoon and evening of the previous day buying camping gear and setting it up in a campsite about ten miles outside Edinburgh. By the time they had bought and pitched the tents, it was getting late and everyone was far too exhausted to do a lengthy technical rehearsal, checking every single lighting and sound cue. So they decided to leave both rehearsals for the following day. That meant they'd had the tech, then the dress rehearsal, and soon they'd be performing for the first time in front of a paying audience.

After they had pitched the tents yesterday, which had proved tricky for some (Will and Connor's tent collapsed twice before Lydia and Georgia lent them a hand), everyone had gathered to enjoy the late-evening sunshine while Jack and Pablo took Alicia back to her B&B. There was no way Alicia's arthritis would let her camp. "I'd be stiff as a corpse each morning," she said, making light of the constant pain in which she lived.

Jack and Pablo had returned with a piping hot fish supper for everyone. They all sat eating happily and swapping camping stories.

"Do you remember when you, me and your dad went camping the summer you were seven,

Georgia?" asked Lydia. "We didn't realise we'd pitched the tent over an underground stream and when it rained in the night the water rose and ran right through the middle of the tent!"

Georgia smiled sadly. Now her parents were getting divorced, she missed those summer family holidays. It was one of the reasons she'd been so pleased about being part of the Swan Circus. She loved her mum, but holidays with just the two of them weren't the same.

After the earlier disaster of the day, everyone was ebullient. The evening was balmy, camping out was different and fun, and hopes were high.

"I can hardly believe we turned it around, everything looked totally hopeless," said Aeysha. "And that makes it seem all the sweeter," she added, popping a large chip smothered with salt and vinegar into her mouth.

"I always knew it was going to be OK," said Eel.

"You didn't seem quite so sure at the time," said Georgia. "Just think, if it hadn't been for Livy, we'd be on a train back to London now, not spending a night under the stars before making our Edinburgh Festival debut." She looked at

Olivia, who had pushed her fish and chips away almost untouched. She seemed to be reading a discarded local newspaper, lost in a story about a break-in at the Tiffany Hotel in which the sapphires of the wife of a famous Scottish actor had been stolen.

"Are you all right, Livy?" asked Aeysha. "You're really quiet."

"I'm just tired," said Olivia stiffly. She was delighted that the Swans were going to be able to perform at the Fringe, but all the pleasure seemed to have gone out of it for her. She couldn't get the conversation she'd overheard out of her head. OK, so Jack had made a stupid mistake over the accommodation, but at some point in his past he had clearly made one that he didn't think could ever be put right. Olivia thought that she knew her dad so well. But maybe she barely knew him at all? What had he done, and how did Alicia know about it? It made Olivia feel as if her whole world had tilted on its axis.

Eel leaned over and nudged her sister. "Livy, if you're not going to eat your chips, can I have them?"

Now it was the next day, and the children were

back at the big top on Calton Hill ready to make their debut. There were two smaller tents behind their large one that served as dressing rooms, one for the boys and one for the girls. There was just half an hour before they would be performing in front of a real audience.

Olivia's phone bleeped with a text from Tom. It simply said: *Break a leg*, which was the way showbusiness people said "Good luck" before a performance.

Georgia peered out of the entrance to the girls' dressing room. She looked at the little makeshift café that they'd made with some rickety tables and chairs bought from a second-hand shop off South Clerk Street. A couple and their two children were being served refreshments by Kasha, but otherwise it was deserted.

"We go up in thirty minutes and there's almost nobody here," she said to Eel, worriedly.

"People will still be dashing here from other shows," said Eel confidently, as she peeped over Georgia's shoulder. "Look!" she said. "There's that woman and her kids from that café where we left a poster. That's nine people. But there'll be more. Jack said that lots of people won't book in advance but just turn up on the day."

"Anyone know how many tickets the Fringe box office has sold?" asked Aeysha. She and Olivia had joined their friends at the tent entrance.

"Yes," said Olivia. "I asked Alicia after the dress rehearsal."

Everyone looked at her expectantly. "So?" said Georgia.

"Nine," said Olivia flatly.

"Oh," said Eel, sounding like a balloon deflating. The minutes ticked by and they took it in turns to check the box office. It was deserted. Not a person in sight.

"Maybe the wrong time is printed in the Fringe programme?" said Georgia, but she knew it wasn't. They had all read the entry so many times. After a few minutes, they heard Pablo announcing that the show was about to start and the tiny audience trickled into the big top.

Jack came and got the children from their dressing tents, pulling on his dark-blue cloak as he walked towards them. He gathered all of them together.

"Right," he said. "Are you all ready? The

Swan Circus is about to make its debut, and let's make it a glorious one!"

"But there's almost nobody here," said Kylie. "There are more of us in the cast than there are in the audience."

A few other people murmured tetchily, too. Connor O'Toole mentioned something about a showbiz rule that meant you didn't have to do a show if the cast outnumbered the audience. Will said he didn't think that applied to the Edinburgh Fringe. Aeysha said that one of her many cousins had been in a show with only one person in the audience, who'd turned out to be a critic from a national newspaper. This had been a disaster because the show required a lot of audience participation and everyone knew critics hated audience participation. The show had been given one star.

It was so disappointing. Everyone was tired after the dramas of the day before and from not being used to sleeping under canvas. Some people had been awake since 4 a.m. when the first birds started singing. It had been an incredibly long day and now they were about to debut before an audience of nine. After all their hard work it was completely disheartening.

"I think we should cancel," said Kylie mutinously.

"I know the audience is small," said Jack. "But this is the first preview. It will take time to build an audience." Although his voice was bright, his eyes looked so defeated and worried that Olivia felt a sudden surge of protective love for him. It didn't matter what he had done in the past. He was her dad and she loved him. She glared at Kylie.

"It doesn't matter if there are nine or nine hundred people," she said fiercely. "Of course we're going to do the show. We're Swans. For Swans, the show always goes on and we've got to be the best we can be."

Jack looked at her gratefully. "Liv's right," he said. "If we give those nine people a really great show, they'll tell all their friends, who will come and tell their friends. That way the audience will grow."

"Great," muttered somebody at the back. "So by the end of the run we might have a whole thirty-six punters." A few people laughed.

"Nobody is forcing you to do it," said Olivia hotly. "If you can't be bothered, you could just pack up and go home. But I'm staying, and I'm going to do a show."

"Us too!" shouted Georgia, Aeysha, Will and some of the others. "Of course we want to do the show!" So many people yelled their agreement that there was no need to take a vote. Even Kylie was swept up in the moment.

"Good," said Jack. "Then let's make it a brilliant one."

They all walked quickly towards the big top as the music began, their excitement rising. Jack squeezed Olivia's hand. "Thanks for helping me out, Liv. I know I can always trust you to support me, both up on the wire and down on the ground."

Olivia looked up into her father's open face and tired blue eyes and suddenly forgot all her suspicions. Whatever he had done was in the past. Perhaps one day he would tell her about it. But for the time being he needed all the support he could get and she was going to give it to him. And she knew that once the show began and the adrenalin kicked in, everyone would give the performance of their lives.

"Everything's going to be OK, Dad," she said. "*Enchantment* is going to be a huge success."

Chapter Six

The show was heading towards its finale. In the middle of the big top, Georgia, Kylie and some of the others, dressed in various shades of green, were swinging round and round, on great multicoloured skeins of material known as silks. They were wearing ballet shoes and were poised en pointe. The effect was beautiful, as if a forest of slender, delicate trees were swaying gracefully in the wind under a series of falling rainbows. The music reached its dreamy climax as the girls spun faster and faster, until it seemed as if they might rise off the ground and take flight. The audience cheered in appreciation, and the Swans moved seamlessly into the very final sequence of the show. The audience were loving every minute. As the show ended and the final cheers died away at last, Olivia and the others ran excitedly into the girls' dressing room.

"It may only have been nine people, but a standing ovation is a standing ovation," said Georgia delightedly. Olivia, who was texting Tom to tell him about it, grinned and nodded.

"They loved it," said Aeysha. "Particularly the silks. I love that bit so much, too. You all look so ethereal. Who would have thought that something so simple as people tumbling and swinging on lengths of material could be so magical?"

"It might look simple," said Georgia, "but I'm hanging on for dear life."

"But you don't look as though you are," said Aeysha. "You make it look easy. The whole sequence makes me feel tingly when I watch it."

"It's because of Kasha's music," said Eel.

"And Pablo's lighting," said Aeysha. "The way it throws shadows against the sides of the tent is brilliant. Really spooky."

"And the way he and Jack have choreographed it all," added Olivia.

"And," finished Eel, "because we're all so brilliant on the silks. Well, at least for beginners."

"Yes," said Alicia, who'd been listening in, amused. "For total beginners, you are all brilliant on the silks. The cleverness is in the way Jack has disguised your very considerable limitations and played to your strengths. There's no one thing that makes that sequence so good, it's the mix of all of them. Take just one element away and it would be distinctly average. The sum is more than the parts. But well done, everyone. I was glad to see you gave it your all, even for such a tiny audience. It's a lovely show. One of the best the Swans have done."

Olivia knew that was high praise coming from Alicia. When Olivia and Eel had first arrived at the Swan, their grandmother had dismissed the circus as having no value and had a grudge against it because it had taken Toni away from her and the London stage. Olivia was just beaming at her gran when the woman from the café came up.

"I just wanted to tell you how much my kids and I enjoyed the show," she said. "I'll be telling all my customers about it. Shame there were so few people here, it was magic!"

"I wish we could magic up some more," said Eel, hopping from foot to foot.

"You don't need magic for that, just a good show. Now you just need to let people know about it," said the café owner. "You need to get busy leafleting and offering half-price tickets. Maybe even give some tickets away. That's what everyone does in the first few days to get an audience and generate word of mouth. It's an investment."

Eel turned a cartwheel in her excitement.

"Mum, I want to learn how to do that," said the café owner's son, who was about Eel's age.

"Me too," said his sister, who was a couple of years older.

"I'll teach you," said Eel, and she started showing them what to do while the woman continued talking to Alicia and Jack, who had come to join them all.

The café owner smiled at Alicia. "It's a pity there's nowhere round here where my kids could learn circus skills. They'd love that." She looked over to where her children were tumbling about with Eel and laughing. "Come on, you two, time to go," she called, and they set off down the hill, calling their goodbyes over their shoulders.

Olivia stared after them. "That's it!" she

said, very suddenly and very loudly.

"That's what?" asked Aeysha, puzzled. "What on earth are you talking about, Livy?"

"She's started rambling," said Eel. "Exhaustion must have softened her brain."

"That's what we need to do!" Olivia's eyes were gleaming.

"But what is the what?" asked Jack, rubbing his eyes. He was very, very tired and there was still work to be done to re-rigg and secure the tent overnight. Although they'd be taking any valuables back to the campsite every evening, he was still concerned that the tent would be vulnerable at night. What they really needed was some overnight security but that was too costly.

"Circus-skills workshops!" said Olivia triumphantly.

Jack's eyes lit up. Alicia's face sharpened too, as if her brain had gone into overdrive.

Olivia continued. "We give free circus-skills workshops for kids who come to the shows. If the parents buy a family ticket, their children get a free workshop before the show or even the next day."

Alicia and Jack looked at each other with

mounting excitement. "I've said it before, and I'll say it again: Liv, you are a genius!" cried Jack.

"I think that's going too far, Dad," said Eel with a grin, "but it *is* a fab idea. Let's do it."

The next morning Olivia and the others were out early on the Royal Mile. They were giving out Swan Circus flyers that were so freshly printed they still smelled woody and inky. Olivia gave them a surreptitious sniff and decided that it was the scent of optimism. They'd had five thousand leaflets printed that morning at what had seemed such vast expense that Alicia had commented drily that clearly the only people getting rich in Edinburgh during August were printers.

Now the Swans were out in force on the streets before the afternoon performance, handing out the leaflets and trying to persuade people to come and see the Swan Circus. Some of the cast had gone down to the half-price Fringe ticket booth and others were out in costume, wandering the streets looking for likely punters.

Alicia advised them only to give the flyers to people who showed genuine interest. Eel had already persuaded a party of Guides and their leader to come to the afternoon show. The leaflets offered a two-for-one deal, but they'd also had a smaller number of flyers printed that offered completely free seats, as well as flyers for the circus-skills workshop.

"We ought to be heading back to Calton Hill," called Aeysha. They'd all agreed to meet back at the big top at 2 p.m. to run through some parts of the show that needed polishing up a bit.

"Coming," said Olivia.

They passed a newspaper seller, who was shouting out the headline news. "Daring jewel theft at Devlin Hotel. Thief gets away with priceless horde. Read all about it!"

"Hey, that's the hotel where we saw those sisters and their dog yesterday," said Georgia.

"Expect they were staking the place out," said Olivia, laughing. They walked to the top of the Mound and started down the steps.

"Look," said Olivia, pointing to where a crowd had gathered. "It's that boy-magician we saw yesterday. Let's go and see if he's got a different routine."

She ran down the steps as Aeysha called out, "We don't have time!" after her. By the time she and Georgia caught Olivia up, she and Eel had already threaded their way to the front of the thong.

"I want you to choose a number," the boy was saying. "Any number, maybe a favourite number, but for your own sakes make it a fairly simple one because you are going to do some arithmetic with it." The boy paused. "Right, are you all thinking of a number?" The crowd nodded. "Don't tell anyone your number, it's your own personal secret number, and for you it's going to be a magic number. Now double your number." He paused briefly again. "Now add fourteen." Some people, including Eel, frowned as they did the adding up.

The boy continued. "What I need you to do now is to divide this new number in two." Lots of people in the crowd were frowning in concentration. "Almost there," he said. "I promise, your brains will stop hurting soon. Now take away your original number from your new number, and you will all be left with another number. And I can tell you that the number you are all left with is the number seven."

A ripple of amazement ran through the crowd and everyone applauded. The boy bowed several times. As the crowd drifted away, he started to pack up his things.

"Hello again," said Olivia. The boy looked up and grinned. Once again, Olivia was struck by how much he looked like Jack.

"That's clever but it's not really magic, is it?" said Georgia shyly.

The boy smiled again. "You're right, it's more maths than magic," he said. "But most people don't really want to know how or why it works. They just want to be amazed." He leaned forward and plucked an apple from behind Georgia's ear before taking a bite out of it. Georgia looked so astonished that they all laughed.

"See, it's a real apple, but you've allowed yourself to be deceived into thinking that it was behind your ear. What you saw and what you think you saw are two different things. The eyes and the brain play tricks on each other."

"You're the best magician I've ever seen," said Aeysha.

"Are you in a show?" asked Olivia.

The boy shook his head and looked sad. "I wish," he said bitterly, and he continued packing up his things.

"You could be in ours. You'd fit right in,"

said Olivia, carried away by her enthusiasm, and she shoved a leaflet for a free ticket in his hand.

Aeysha and Georgia glanced at each other. They thought Olivia was being overhasty in offering the boy a chance to be part of the Swan Circus. "Livy…" said Aeysha uncertainly.

The boy looked at the leaflet and a strange look flitted across his face. He whispered, "A circus? You're part of a circus?"

Olivia nodded eagerly.

"I've never even been allowed to see a circus," he said, "so I can guarantee I'd never be allowed to actually be in one," and he strode away without even saying goodbye.

They stared after him.

"That was a bit odd," said Georgia. "He seemed really upset, almost angry."

Olivia shrugged. "Does he remind you of anyone?" she asked, her voice casual.

"Um, not really," said Georgia. "Oh, maybe – that bloke who does magic on the telly? But that boy's better. He should have his own TV show."

Aeysha was still watching the boy as he disappeared through the crowd. "I know who he looked like just then," she said. "It was the same body language. He looked exactly like Eel when she's in a terrible strop."

Eel gasped indignantly. "Strop? Me? Never!" Everyone burst out laughing, except Olivia, who studied her little sister thoughtfully.

Chapter Seven

That afternoon, they had almost fifty people in the audience and agreed it was a great deal better than nine. Lots of children had signed up for the free circus-skills workshop the following morning, which was encouraging, too. But Olivia could see from the grown-ups' worried glances that fifty people wasn't nearly enough, particularly as most of them were on half-price or free tickets. But again the audience had been really enthusiastic and at the end they had clapped and cheered, and some had even stamped their feet. Or forty-nine of them had…

When Olivia had finished her turn on the high-wire and was taking her bow, she thought that she'd heard a distinct boo among the cheers. It was unsettling and had made her heart beat

73

faster. She had glanced round to see if anybody else had heard it, but they were all smiles; she anxiously scanned the faces of the small crowd but she couldn't see where the boo might have come from. Perhaps she had imagined it?

And perhaps she hadn't been all that good? She did feel tired, as the last few days had taken their toll. She always knew when she was at her best on the wire because her mind emptied of everything except an awareness of her own body. She knew that Eel felt the same when she was dancing really well.

Jack always said that to walk the wire properly you had to leave anything you didn't need behind on the ground. No, she hadn't been at her best; even as she dismounted she had seen Jack's slightly raised eyebrow and she knew that she had been sloppy, somehow remaining earthbound even though she had been up in the air. Jack never expected anything less than one hundred per cent from anyone, but particularly from Olivia. Although she expected no less of herself, it sometimes felt as if Jack wanted even more.

She knew why her father was pushing her so hard. A lot of the show had been created to specifically disguise the fact that most of the Swans were beginners when it came to circus skills, although their dance training meant that they were all exceptionally lithe and strong and so had a head-start. Olivia knew that the core of the show relied on her and her dad's and Pablo's genuine skill and talent and many years of hard training. Even Eel's prowess at acrobatics was really window dressing, although the crowd loved it when she exploded across the ring, somersaulting and cart-wheeling like a demon. Alicia didn't like it so much, she was always worried that Eel would injure herself and not be able to continue her dance training. Olivia knew that Jack and Pablo had been concerned about the lack of core skills at the heart of the circus, because she had heard them discussing it.

"What we really need is a couple more children with really first-class skills," Jack had said. "It's such a pity that Tom is still in *Peter Pan*. He may not be experienced but he's such a natural on the high-wire."

"The show is good, Jack," replied Pablo. "And we can hide the holes. If we are very cunning, most people won't even notice that our little ducklings haven't been doing circus all their lives. And Livy, she will not let us down. She is such a professional. She carries the show."

Olivia had immediately texted Tom to tell him what Jack and Pablo had said about him.

Tom had replied straightaway. "*Aw, shucks. But you know what they say, pride comes before a fall, and it's an awfully long way down from the high-wire.*"

Olivia couldn't help feeling proud that she too was such an essential part of the Swan Circus, but it also felt like a bit of a burden. At least today it did when her mind was so full. She watched the audience drifting away or chatting with Alicia and Jack, who were trying to engage with as many people as possible after the afternoon show, like good hosts saying goodbye to party guests.

She wondered who it was in the audience who had booed. Only a professional who knew a great deal about circus performance would have noticed that she hadn't quite nailed the routine.

Aeysha and Georgia came up to see if she wanted to go into town between shows. They set off, handing out a few leaflets to families on the way.

"It went well, didn't it?" said Aeysha happily.

"Did you hear anything odd after my tightrope routine?" asked Olivia.

"What do you mean, odd?" asked Georgia.

Olivia found she couldn't quite bring herself to explain. She shrugged, but her face was anxious and she felt on edge.

"All I heard was the sound of people enjoying themselves," said Aeysha.

They stopped to buy sandwiches and then wandered into Greyfriars Kirkyard. They were just starting to cross the path towards a tree so they could sit in the shade when the girl in the yellow dress came running along the path at full tilt, her dog close on her heels. She clearly didn't intend to stop, so they stood back to let her pass, but she didn't even thank them. Instead, when she saw Olivia, she looked surprised, scowled and then stuck out her tongue. She clearly hadn't forgotten their encounter at the magic show. The collie gave a little woof as if in thanks and raced after her.

"Did you see that!" said Olivia, outraged, as they settled themselves under the tree. But she gasped as the same thickset man they had seen on the steps at the Mound suddenly appeared through the other gate.

"I think he's the reason she was in a hurry," said Georgia.

"There's something really odd about all this," said Aeysha. "You don't often see kids being chased through the streets by grown-ups, do you? Livy, did you ever tell Jack about what you saw in the garage?"

Olivia blushed. "No, I forgot. I've had other things on my mind and so has Dad."

"I think you should," said Aeysha. "Maybe those girls are in some kind of trouble?"

"P'haps they're runaways?" said Georgia. "That could be why they're sleeping in a garage."

The man lumbered towards them. He was breathing heavily as if he'd been running and his forehead was shiny with sweat. "You seen a girl?" he asked. "Dark hair. Yellow dress. Dog." He gave what he clearly hoped was a charming smile. "My niece," he added, and there was a sorrowful edge to his voice. "The wee one and her big sister, both a bundle of trouble. They've been nothing but a pain since I took them in and gave them a home after my poor sister died." He shook his head sadly. "But they're poor wee orphans and I'm just trying to do my best by them. But my best is not good enough for them. Na'er a thank you. All they do is keep running away." He put his hand theatrically on the left-hand side of his chest. "It's breaking my old heart. If you tell me where she went you'd be doing her and me a favour. I want us to be a family again." His eyes watered. The girls were so embarrassed they didn't know where to look.

He seemed so pitiful that Georgia began: "I think she—" when Aeysha butted in firmly and said, "We haven't seen her. Sorry."

A shadow of something that might have been fury passed across the man's face as if he was certain they were lying, but he quickly composed his features, thanked them and hurried away.

"Why didn't you tell him that we did see her?" asked Georgia. "He was so sad about his nieces. I thought he was going to cry."

"Or maybe he's some kind of con man who's very good at acting," said Aeysha tartly. "How do you know he's even their uncle?"

"He's definitely right about the lack of manners," said Olivia.

"Look," continued Aeysha, "I know that

girl's really rude, but maybe she and her sister have got a very good reason for running away from him? Maybe it would be really awful for them if he found them? One thing I do know is that the girl's dog doesn't like him. He tripped him up on the Mound, and if that clever dog doesn't like him, that's good enough for me."

A little over an hour later Olivia stood just outside the big top, ready to make her entrance. There were at least a hundred people in the tent for the evening performance. Things were looking up, but Olivia knew that the big test would be whether audiences would still come when they had to fork out the full price for the tickets. She had heard Alicia on the phone to the arts desks of some of the newspapers trying to get them to send critics early in the hope that good reviews would help.

Jack's tired, tense face made it clear that the circus was a big financial drain. "We're haemorrhaging money," he'd murmured once, realising that he needed to make yet another visit to the cashpoint. They had expected to eat most meals cheaply in the rented house – Lydia was a great cook who knew how to eke out a budget – but cooking every day for a large number of people at the campsite just wasn't practical, so they were surviving on sandwiches and expensive takeaways. Jack's main hope was that he might recover the several thousand pounds he had paid the scammer. He'd reported it to the police and they were investigating, but even if they caught the man responsible there was no guarantee that Jack would get his money back.

"I'd dearly love to get my hands on the swindler," said Jack, after yet another fruitless trip to the police station. "When I've got more time I'm going to do a bit of my own investigating."

Olivia watched as the scene from *A Midsummer Night's Dream* came to its conclusion. The show was going really well tonight. The audience loved the opening with its excerpt from *Swan Lake* with Aeysha, Georgia and Eel wearing long-necked swan masks fashioned out of wire. Their pleasure turned to wonder at the carnival of animals that followed. There was a performing seal and a roaring tiger that could be seen getting the better of his clownish tamer (played by Jazz with a long fake moustache).

The animals were *Lion King*-style puppets that included a clever basketwork elephant that had been made in school as part of an art and design project. It was manipulated by the children and lumbered majestically around the ring to the strains of "Nellie the Elephant". The elephant stopped to allow the children in the audience to reach over the side of the ring and pat his trunk and William Todd enjoyed squirting them from his trunk using a concealed water squirter.

Olivia scanned the members of the audience laughing at the fairies, who were dressed in ragged tutus and boots so that they looked like ethereal street urchins. They were leading away Connor O' Toole, who was playing Bottom, and who was a natural clown. He was playing to the crowd, scratching his large ears and braying loudly. His performance brought the house down. Suddenly, the music became louder. Emmy and Daisy, on roller skates as they played the fairies Cobweb and Mustard Seed, weaved dizzying circles around Bottom, spinning so fast that it made you believe that they might actually take off.

In just a few seconds, Olivia would be on. She stood on tiptoes ready to run out into the bright lights of the ring and as she did so she felt something lick her hand. She looked down and there was the black-and-white collie dog looking up at her. She wondered what he was doing here, and whether that meant that the girl was around, too. She remembered that she still hadn't told Jack about what she'd seen in the garage. She vowed to mention it immediately after the show.

"Hello, boy," said Olivia, giving the dog a pat. He looked up at her mournfully with his big intelligent eyes and offered her a paw. "Do you like the circus?" She laughed because it almost looked as if the dog was nodding. "You are such a clever boy."

But then she heard Pablo yelling, "Get on, Livy, you're going to miss your cue!"

Flustered, Olivia ran into the ring and started climbing the tower. Her heart was thumping, and she could see Jack already on the wire. As she reached the top of the tower and stepped out on to the wire, she gazed for just a moment at the audience, their faces quite clear in the lights of the big top. Her eye fell on a figure in the middle of the fifth row: the boy-magician was sat all alone with empty seats on either side of him. He had a rapturous look on his face, as if he was having the best night of his life. She hoped he'd stay behind after the show to see her and her friends. She really felt a connection with him and wanted to talk to him some more. She glanced at him again, and for a split second she didn't see the boy, she saw Jack. The resemblance was so great that they could be father and son...

Father and son! Olivia's brain began to whirl as she stepped out on the wire. She knew that she had to concentrate but her mind was in turmoil. She looked at Jack, balancing at the other end of the wire. He was frowning because she had missed her cue. She stuck out her chin defiantly as she began to move towards him. She heard the crowd give a little "Ooh" as she reached Jack and he raised her up on to his shoulders with one graceful movement.

When she had been little and Jack had lifted her like this, she'd always felt as if she were a doll in the palm of a giant. He was so strong, so effortless in the way that he did it, that it never even crossed her mind that he might drop her. But now, as she started to stand up on his shoulders, she began to feel insecure.

She lost concentration, and as soon as she did, she started to wobble.

For a moment, it seemed certain they would fall, but Jack took control and held her firmly by the ankles. Olivia regained her balance just in time. But she was shaken. She didn't normally wobble.

"Concentrate," she told herself sternly as she held her position. But she couldn't get the boy out of her head. She stole another glance at him; the spotlights meant that she could no longer see his face clearly. She descended to the wire and as she did so she heard another boo amid the clapping. She could see that Jack had heard it, too, but unlike her he had taken it good-naturedly.

"I think we both deserved that," he whispered wryly. Olivia knew that her dad was just being kind. She was the one who had lost concentration. They moved to opposite ends of the wire. A balancing rod in hand, Olivia began a sequence in which she walked along the wire towards Jack, swaying out far to one side so she was perched on one leg and then to the other. It looked really perilous but Olivia found it as easy as walking along a wall. It was just a question of being aware of your centre of gravity. She caught sight of Jack watching her closely and for a split second it was as if she was seeing the boy again. Could he be Jack's son?

No, it was impossible. The boy was clearly younger than her and yet he was older than Eel. Snippets from the conversation she had overheard played in her mind: *I saw Alfie's birth announced in a newspaper...I feel terrible that I've never even seen him. He must be about ten now..."* She continued walking towards the end of the wire, lost in her thoughts. Suddenly, she blundered into something. She heard Jack cry out, the audience gasp and then she was all alone on the wire and there was just a space where Jack should be. White-faced and shaking, Olivia looked down. From somewhere in the crowd she heard a loud boo. Then she gave a huge sob and began climbing down the tower as fast as she could.

Chapter Eight

"What on earth were you thinking about, Liv?" asked Jack gently. The two of them were sitting alone on the grass outside the big top. Everybody else was inside, going through with Pablo how they would run the first circus-skills workshop, which would be starting in just over half an hour. But Jack had wanted to talk to Olivia and this was the first chance he'd had since the fall last night.

Olivia could hardly bear to remember the moment when she had watched Jack falling. It seemed to happen in slow motion. She felt a rush of shame. She had allowed herself to be distracted and had almost killed her own father. If he hadn't landed on one of the mattresses below he might have died or been seriously injured, and it would have been all her fault. One mistake, one tiny lapse in concentration, and she would have had to live with the consequences for the rest of her life. She shivered.

As soon as it was apparent that Jack had landed like a cat and was totally fine, Kasha and the band struck up again and the show had continued. The audience was galvanised, as if the tumble from the wire had made it realise that what it was watching was real and genuinely risky, not just a showy pretence. Jack had even insisted that he and Olivia did the final *Tempest* sequence. He had been extraordinary in that scene, quite electrifying, as if the fall had pushed him on to even greater daring.

But Olivia had seen her father looking at her in a way she had never seen before. He looked wary, as if he didn't quite trust her any more. Remembering this now, she felt so ashamed, and began to cry hot tears.

Jack held her hand. "Liv, chick, we need to talk about this. Analyse what happened, so we can make sure it never happens again."

Olivia nodded miserably. She wished he would be angrier with her. His gentle understanding just made things worse.

"Do you know why you lost focus?" persisted Jack.

Olivia stared at her dad. She couldn't possibly tell him that she had been wondering whether he had been unfaithful to her mother and if she and Eel had a secret half-brother. She felt drained and miserable. If only she had never heard that conversation when she had been in the portaloo, her life would have just gone on as before. But then maybe that life would have been based on a lie?

She remembered how, when she and Eel had first moved in with Alicia, she had accused her grandmother of entirely abandoning them after Toni's death. Alicia had said nothing to defend herself. But then one day when Olivia was looking for some sticky tape she had opened a dusty old drawer in the bureau in the living room and discovered that it was stuffed full of old letters. They'd been written by Alicia to Jack, desperately trying to find out where he and the children were, but they had been returned to her undelivered because the circus was always on the move across Europe.

It had made Olivia realise that what she'd thought was true and what was actually true were two entirely different things.

Jack was waiting patiently for her answer. "I don't know, Dad," she said. "I can't explain it. It just happened. I know that's no excuse. I'm really, really sorry."

"Well, fortunately there was no harm done," said Jack, "but it mustn't happen again, Liv. We've got to be able to trust each other completely out there on the wire. We've got to look after each other, and last night you weren't looking after yourself or me, you were completely lost in your own thoughts. I never want to see you up there again in that state, because if it's going to happen again we can't continue to be partners. I can't risk it, for either your sake or mine. Or the audience's. I know what it's like not to trust your partner, and I don't want to go there again."

Olivia felt a stab of pain in her heart. "What happened?" she asked hesitantly.

Jack sighed. "I was very young. It was the year after your mum and I met. Getting away had seemed the best thing to do, so we were in Spain. I met a tightrope walker there; Nicu was a Romanian married to a Scottish girl called Cora, who was a former gymnast turned contortionist. She was lovely, but she'd had such a sad life. Orphaned at a young age, and then brought up by her aunt, I think. Anyway, Nicu was a good few years older than me. He was the best high-wire walker I've ever seen, and completely fearless. It was like he belonged in the air.

"He already had a little girl about four and Cora was expecting again. Toni was just pregnant with you at the time. So it was natural that the four of us became friends, and after a while, Nicu suggested that he and I did a double act together. We both needed the work, but I knew I should never have said yes."

"But if he was so good, why didn't you want to be his partner?" asked Olivia.

"Because he had a reckless streak. He always pushed everything too far and took unnecessary risks. Performers like that always work solo, because however talented they are nobody wants to work with them. They are a danger to themselves and other people. You only want to be on the wire with someone you trust, someone who will always be ready to catch you if you fall."

"Did something terrible happen?"

Jack nodded. "We were in Seville. It was the third performance of the day and we were all tired. But Nicu was fired up. He wanted to try something new at the next performance. But I thought it was a bad idea. We hadn't rehearsed it enough; I didn't feel at all confident. Nicu agreed that we'd stick to the usual routine. But as soon as I got out there on the wire I sensed that he was excited. His eyes were glittering. Then suddenly, he launched into the new act. I didn't have any choice but to go with him – you can't stop to have an argument with someone when you're both suspended in mid-air on the wire. He was inspired, extraordinary. I fumbled through the routine as best I could, drenched in sweat, just desperate to get to the end in one piece. And we were nearly there, so close to safety. Nicu flipped on to his hands on the wire. It was amazing, and it was supposed to be the end of the show.

"But the crowd was going wild, and it just seemed to egg him on. He stood back up on the wire, took a bow, quietened the audience down with his hands and then he just launched into a series of flips along the wire. I'd never seen anything like it, before or since. He was going so fast he was just a blur."

"What happened?" whispered Olivia.

Jack's face looked pained, remembering the awful scene. "He flipped perfectly, exquisitely along the wire. But he didn't stop. It was as if he was possessed. He just ran out of wire and cartwheeled on into thin air. He hit the ground with a hideous thud, his body flung out in a star shape, arms and legs flailing slightly as if they still thought he was cartwheeling."

"Did he die?" breathed Olivia.

"No," said Jack grimly, "but he never walked again. Cora went into premature labour and gave birth to another little girl."

"What happened to him and his family?"

Jack shook his head. "I don't know. We lost touch. I'd already met Pablo and we started to cook up some stunts, like the one at the Eiffel Tower in Paris. Toni and I left Spain soon after. From time to time I'd hear something about Nicu. He was scraping a living together by teaching, but he wasn't a well man and it was tough. I think eventually the family may have gone back to Romania, or maybe they came to Scotland. I don't know. I feel guilty that I didn't try and stay in touch. I often wonder what happened to Cora and those two little girls and how they survived."

Olivia swallowed. "I won't lose my concentration again," she whispered.

"I don't think you will, either." Jack smiled. "I trust you."

"And I trust you, Dad," said Olivia, but as she said the words she wondered if it was really true. The doubt that had crept into their relationship felt like a tiny drop of poison polluting a clear blue lake. She knew she had to ask him straight.

"Dad," she said slowly, "you don't have any other children, do you, besides Eel and me?"

For a second, Jack just stared at her, a mixture of astonishment and puzzlement in his eyes, and then he threw back his head and roared with laughter.

"What on earth made you ask that?" he said. "No, Liv, as far as I'm aware I have no other children. You and Eel are quite enough."

Jack stopped laughing when he saw something was still troubling his daughter, but at that moment Georgia ran up and said that the circus-skills workshop was about to start and they were needed immediately.

Jack stood up and put out his hand to Olivia. "Come on, partner, let's go teach some tightrope walking."

Chapter Nine

"This is such fun!" said Georgia, chasing after yet another ball that Becky, the café owner's daughter, had dropped. Pablo and Will were teaching her group to juggle, and Georgia had dropped almost as many balls as Becky. But everyone was enjoying themselves.

Pablo had planned the session really well, aiming to make sure that all the children left the workshop feeling that they had achieved something. The Swans had started the session with an impressive skipping demonstration, showing off their fabulous footwork from years of dance training. Kylie and Eel could skip and tap dance at the same time, which had attracted admiring "Oohs" and "Aahs" from the watching children. Although some of the local boys had initially complained that skipping was for girls, they had soon joined in when Kasha and his mate, Jazz, showed how fast and hard they could skip.

It was a clever move on Pablo's part. Everybody can skip a bit so the children quickly made progress and by the end everyone had a new trick they could show off in the playground. Later, he planned to show them how to build the first couple of layers of a *castell*, the human towers that hailed from the Catalan region of Spain.

Now, under the watchful eye of Alicia, Eel was teaching a small group of girls how to do a perfect cartwheel and Pablo was teaching simple juggling. At one side of the ring, Jack and Olivia were setting up a wire just centimetres off the ground so those who wanted to could get a taste of tightrope walking. As she was securing the wire at one end, Olivia heard a little bark. She turned around to find the collie dog, wagging its tail and panting happily.

"Hello, boy," she said, ruffling the fur on his head. "Do you want to learn circus skills?" He raised a paw to her and she shook it, laughing. The dog licked her hand. Olivia glanced up, and saw the two sisters sitting on the side of the ring. She was still feeling wary of the younger girl but she knew it was important to make everyone feel welcome. It was part of the Swans' training. Besides, she was curious about the sisters. So she gave both girls a little smile and wave. The elder girl waved back, but the younger one scowled and just went back to the intense conversation she was having with her sister. Olivia gritted her teeth and ran over to them anyway.

As she did so, she caught a snatch of what the girl was saying. "It's perfect, Tati. It's so lucky you got one of those leaflets. He'd never think of looking for us here. Not with a bunch of amateur circus kids…" There was a scorn in her voice that made Olivia prickle with annoyance. What did she know about the circus, anyway?

The older sister looked anxious. "But what if he finds out? It could bring down trouble on them all…" She broke off when she realised that Olivia was hovering nearby.

Olivia took a deep breath and tried to be nice. "Hi, I'm Olivia," she said, and she added shyly: "I remember you from the Mound. The magic show…."

"I remember you, too," said the younger

girl, with a shrug that suggested she hadn't forgotten their argument.

"I'm Tatiana. But every one calls me Tati," said the elder girl quickly, "and this is my little sister, Evie."

"I'm not little," said Evie, glaring at her sister. "I'm thirteen."

"Do you want to join in?" asked Olivia. "You could try some juggling, if you like." She pointed to the other end of the tent. The younger girl just stared at her stonily and shook her head. Her elder sister smiled apologetically, seeming embarrassed by her sister's rudeness.

"Oh, whatever," said Olivia, running out of patience. She went back to helping Jack with the wire. Why would anyone bother to come to a circus-skills workshop if they didn't want to join in?

"Hey, it's those girls again," said Aeysha, coming over to see whether Olivia and Jack were ready to start the tightrope walking session.

"I know," replied Olivia. "I spoke to them. At least the older one tries to be pleasant but the younger one is just plain rude."

At that moment, Becky dropped two of her balls again and a third shot off in an arc. The collie chased after it, caught it on his nose and started bouncing it up and down with a skill that would have made a World Cup-winning footballer jealous. Everyone clapped.

"That dog's amazing!" said Georgia. "That dog's so clever." Evie gave a whistle and the collie raced around the ring, leapt over the barrier and landed in her lap, where he started to lick her face vigorously. The children cheered and ran over. Even Olivia couldn't resist following, the dog was so loveable.

"What's his name?" Aeysha asked Evie.

"Harry," replied Evie, her eyes sparkling. Pride and pleasure in her dog had transformed her face from its usual watchful state. It was as if she had let down her guard against the world. "After Houdini. Cos he's a real escape artist."

"Just like you," said Tati. Both sisters had Scottish accents but with a trace of something else that Olivia couldn't quite place. The sisters glanced at each other as if sharing a memory.

"Did you train him yourself?" asked Georgia.

Evie grinned and nodded. "My auntie Zsa Zsa taught me how to do it. She's a professional animal trainer. She's the best."

"Maybe she could train my dog? He's a Jack Russell and he's very naughty," said Georgia.

Tati shook her head sadly. "We don't know where she lives any more. We haven't seen or heard from her for a couple of years. She might even be dead."

The Swans gasped.

"No she isn't; I know she isn't!" said Evie desperately. "She can't be, not Auntie Zsa Zsa. She's too full of life."

Olivia saw the same mix of vulnerability and defiance in the girl's face that she'd noticed on the Mound steps. She remembered what she'd glimpsed through the garage window and wanted to ask them why they were living there, but she could hardly just blurt out a question like that.

"Do you and your family live in Edinburgh or are you just here for the Festival?" she asked, as casually as she could.

Tati looked sad. "Our mum and dad are— Ow!" she cried, as Evie kicked her and told her to shut up.

Just then, Jack called out: "So who wants to try tightrope walking?" The Swans and some of the other children whooped and ran towards the low wire, while others drifted over to Pablo, who was going to show them how to build *castells*. Olivia walked a little way behind the girls, trying to text Tom quickly before the tightrope session began. She stopped still when she heard Evie hiss angrily at her sister.

"Stop talking so much, Tati. You'll be broadcasting our business to everyone next, not just that nosy circus girl. We shouldn't trust anyone. Look what happened with Mitch."

"I was just trying to be nice, Evie," replied Tati. "If we're going to get them to trust us, you're going to have to be a lot less rude." She sighed. "You used to be such a sweet little thing, Evie."

"I'm trying to be tough, Tati," snapped her sister. "If there's one thing I've learned over the last few months it's that only the tough survive. We can't rely on anybody except each other."

Olivia couldn't stop a sneeze escaping, and Evie and Tati fell abruptly silent.

"Liv!" Jack signalled that he needed her to help him, and as she ran back down into the ring she remembered where she had heard that name before: the man who had swindled Jack out of his money was also called Mitch! If Evie,

Tati and Houdini were living in the garages at Jekyll Street and knew someone called Mitch, then maybe they had some connection to the scam? Maybe they could tell Jack where to find Mitch?

She couldn't wait to tell Jack what she had discovered, but it'd have to wait until after the workshop. She felt a tingle of anticipation in her tummy. She leapt on to the wire and gave a graceful demonstration of wire-walking that brought admiring glances.

"Who wants to have a go?" asked Jack and every single child in the group put up a hand. They formed an excited, unruly queue, and one by one he and Olivia helped them up on to the wire. Most of the children wobbled and would have fallen if they hadn't grabbed wildly at Olivia and Jack's outstretched hands. But one boy, who'd done horseriding, had excellent balance and successfully managed a few steps before he became over-confident and fell off. Everyone clapped.

"Come on, Liv, give us another demonstration," said Jack, smiling proudly at his daughter. Olivia leapt on to the wire and danced along it with such grace it was as if her feet barely touched it. She jumped off, and saw Evie staring at her, a small smile playing around her lips. The girl had moved to the back of the group gathered around the wire as if she was unable to keep away from it.

Everyone else applauded, but Evie just carried on staring at Olivia, an unimpressed gleam in her eye. Olivia bristled. She'd like to see her do better! She may make it look easy, but it took years and years of dedication to walk the wire well.

"Would you like to try?" she asked, and there was a challenge in her eyes. She knew she was being a little bit mean, but she was rather looking forward to seeing the rude girl take a tumble.

Evie looked Olivia up and down, and shrugged. She glanced at the wire and the curly haired boy who was teetering along it, supported by Jack and Aeysha. "That's for babies," she sneered.

"I bet you won't say that when you get on it," said Olivia. "Bet you won't be able to walk from one end to the other without falling off."

Evie scrutinised her coolly with an infuriatingly confident smile. "Bet I can."

Olivia rather admired the girl's bravura. "Go on, then," she said, and she knew her words were like a dare. The girl held her gaze boldly for just a moment, and then she turned and ran very fast towards the tower at the side of the ring and started climbing it with speed and agility.

"Evie," called Tati, looking worried.

Olivia gritted her teeth. No one was allowed to go near the high-wire that she and Jack used for the circus performances. Why did that girl have to be so annoying? "Evie, come back," she shouted, certain that as soon as the girl realised how high off the ground the wire was, she'd come straight back down.

But Evie just continued to climb up towards the wire. Olivia suddenly felt alarmed, and ran towards the tower. If anything happened to the girl, she would be partly to blame.

"Come back down!" she shouted. "Don't be such an idiot!"

Olivia's shout made Jack and Pablo look round. As soon as they realised what was happening, they raced towards the tower. Pablo overtook Olivia and was up after Evie like a monkey. But she had a good head start and she had almost reached the top.

"Come down!" yelled Jack desperately. "What on earth does she think she's playing at?" he said to Olivia, whose heart had begun to thump so hard it seemed to be trying to burst right out of her chest. Olivia shook her head hopelessly.

Evie had reached the top of the ladder and was now standing where the wire began, stretched taut across to the other tower. Olivia waited for Evie to take in the dizzying drop to the ground, and come back down. But instead she did something that made Olivia feel as if somebody had removed all the bones in her legs. She stuck her tongue out at Olivia, and then she stepped out on to the wire.

Jack put his head in his hands, and Pablo shouted, "Noooooooooo!" Evie completely ignored them. She took another step, as if testing the wire, and then sashayed along it as if she hadn't a care in the world. When she got to the other end she turned back, flipped on to her hands and walked along the wire upside down. Down below, the children all clapped and cheered. Then Evie stopped mid-wire, and balanced on both her hands. The children below whooped with delight.

Olivia couldn't believe her eyes. Jack's expression was part fury and part astonishment. Then Evie was back up on her feet, pirouetting along the wire. She reached the tower, rubbed her hands together in a gesture that suggested a job well done, and took a bow. Then she started to climb down.

When she reached the bottom, she was mobbed by everybody. Olivia hung back and watched. She had never seen anything like the display. She felt a mixture of admiration and fury. If Evie had fallen, it would have been the end of her and the Swan Circus.

Olivia followed Jack as he pushed his way through the crowd. Even his back radiated anger. He stopped in front of the girl, who stared at him with a look of both satisfaction and defiance on her face.

"How dare you!" Jack yelled, his voice shaking with a mixture of shock and anger. "You could have been killed! How could you be so reckless? The high-wire isn't something you can just muck about on when you feel like it. Right, tell me where you live. I'm going to take you home, because someone needs to have a word with your parents about your—"

"You're the great Marvello, aren't you," interrupted Evie, in a tone that made it clear that it was a statement, not a question.

Jack was so taken aback by her calm coolness that he nodded. "And you are…?"

"Evenga Purcarete, but everyone calls me Evie. This is my sister Tati."

"Purcarete? You're not Nicu Purcarete's daughter, are you?" Jack gave a little whistle of amazement and then his face broke into a big grin. "What an extraordinary coincidence! I was only telling Liv about your dad this morning, wasn't I, Liv?" He turned to Olivia, who nodded, so livid at Evie's stunt that she couldn't speak.

"Yes, the Magnificent Purcarete. He was the best," said Evie, and her dark eyes shone with pride and unshed tears.

"Ah," said Jack softly. "So he's no longer with us. I'm so sorry, Evie. He was a special talent."

And reckless like his daughter, thought Olivia.

There was an awkward pause, and then Jack asked: "So where's your mum? How is she? I'd love to see her again."

"I'm afraid you can't," said Tati in a quiet, quavering voice. "She died a few weeks ago. Leukaemia." A tear dripped down her cheek. Murmurs of sympathy went round the listening children. Olivia's throat tightened and she thought she might cry, too.

"Evie," said Jack gently, his face serious. "You do realise what you did was unbelievably, unforgiveably dangerous. You can't behave in that reckless way in a circus. You might have hurt other people and you might have been killed if you'd fallen."

"I never fall," said Evie, with a shrug that got Olivia riled up all over again. Evie Purcarete really was one of the most arrogant people she had ever met in her entire life. She expected Jack to say something along the lines of "pride comes before a fall" and read Evie the riot act, but to her surprise a twinkle had crept into his eye.

"Well, Evie, you're certainly not lacking in confidence!" he said. "And from what I've just seen, you have every right to be confident. What you did was wrong, very wrong, but it was a wonderful display. The last time I saw you, you were a bawling scrap of a thing, a tiny little baby. Your father taught you well. If you're interested,

I reckon we might have a spot for you in the Swan Circus."

"Dad!" exclaimed Olivia. How could he just offer a total stranger a job in their circus without asking the rest of them first? In her outrage, she conveniently forgot that she'd done exactly the same thing with the boy-magician. But Jack's hand silenced her, and judging from the admiring, sympathetic looks on the faces of the other Swans, they weren't fussed about the lack of consultation. Evie grinned at Jack and her dark, watchful eyes were suddenly full of light. She looked at her sister, who nodded and smiled.

"We would like that very much," she said.

"Good," said Jack, "because you're the best high-wire walker of your age that I've ever seen."

Olivia felt as if she'd just been slapped. Evie and she were almost the same age, there couldn't be more than a few months between them, and Jack was suggesting that Evie was a better tightrope walker than she was, his own daughter, the person he had been teaching almost since the day she could walk. She felt utterly betrayed. And it felt all the worse because Olivia was now certain that she knew who had booed her during their Swan Circus performances. She felt as though a snake was settling into an uncomfortable coil in her stomach, and as she tried to contain the sandpaper itch in her throat, Olivia realised that she was jealous.

Chapter Ten

"How could he? How could he do such a thing?" raged Georgia. Her face was tear-streaked and her fair skin blotchy from crying. Olivia and Aeysha were sitting just outside the tent that the three of them shared.

"My poor mum!" wailed Georgia. "I'm never going to talk to my dad ever again. He's toast as far as I'm concerned." Her rosebud mouth was set in a mutinous line.

"Oh, Georgia, you don't really mean that," said Aeysha carefully. "I can see that it's really upsetting, and it's a shock, but it's not as if your mum and dad were ever going to get back together again. Your mum seems fine about it; she's only upset because you're so upset. Only the other day you were saying that she was relieved that the divorce was almost through so she'd be able to get on with the rest of her life. You said that she said that she and your dad had both moved on. You even said how much you liked your dad's girlfriend."

"Maybe I did," said Georgia, "but that doesn't mean I want him to marry her and for her to have his baby. It's all too soon."

"But you'll love having a little brother or sister, Georgie," said Aeysha. "You've always said that you wished you had a bigger family and that you weren't an only child. Now you won't be."

"Dad and Leonie and the baby will be a real family. I'll just be the half-sister. The outsider who comes to visit. Since Dad left, Mum and I have only been half a family, like the last couple of bits of stale cake in the tin that nobody wants!" Georgia burst into angry tears again.

Aeysha patted her back, and Olivia drew circular movements with her finger on the inside of Georgia's elbow. It was something that Eel and she did when the other one was really stressed, and they always found it soothing. She knew that if Jack suddenly announced that he was getting married again and having a baby with his new fiancée, she would feel just like Georgia, but she could see that Aeysha was right too.

"Well, I think you're lucky to have two families. You'll be able to choose the bits you like best from both of them. Most of us don't have a choice. We just have to make the best of the family we've got," said Aeysha, who was the eldest girl of seven children and often joked that she liked coming to school because it gave her a rest from the noise and mayhem.

"But you wouldn't want to swap your family for another one, would you?" said Georgia, sniffing.

"Of course not," said Aeysha. "But I also know that one day, when I'm older, I will want to leave them and set out on my own. My brother cried on the day he went away to college and said he didn't want to go, but my mum made him go, even though I knew she was dreading her eldest child leaving home. She said it was the next step in his life and he'd regret it if he didn't take it. Now he loves it, and can't stop talking about uni and his friends when he comes back to visit."

"I'm never going to leave my mum," said

Georgia fiercely. "Not ever!"

Aeysha glanced at Olivia over Georgia's head. "You may say that now, Georgie, but you wouldn't want everything to stay the same for ever. Imagine if your mum still treated you like she did when you were four or if you were never allowed to go up a grade in ballet or got any better at algebra. Although in your case, Georgie, it would be hard to get any better at algebra than you already are."

Georgia gave a pleased, embarrassed little smile. It was true she was very good at maths, just like her accountant father.

Olivia knew that Aeysha was right and that change could be a good thing. She had hated leaving the travelling circus and coming to the Swan but it had been the best thing that ever happened to her. But maybe Aeysha's willingness to embrace change came from the fact that she felt so secure in her own family, or the clan as she called them, a great network of cousins, aunts and uncles as well as her own siblings.

Olivia didn't have a clue who her great-grandparents were, and as far as she was aware she didn't have any cousins at all. Her mum had been an only child, and Jack had never mentioned any brothers and sisters. In fact, now she thought about it, Jack never mentioned much about his childhood at all, except that his parents had died within months of each other when he was seventeen and he'd got his first job in a circus shortly after. "I was an orphan," he'd said. "The circus became my family."

"Maybe," ventured Olivia, "family seems more precious when you don't have much of it, like Georgia and me. You want to hold on tight to the bit you've got."

Aeysha laughed good-naturedly. "That might be true. My family love each other but they're always falling out with each other and having feuds."

"What sort of feuds?" asked Georgia, who had long stopped crying. She was fascinated by Aeysha's big family and loved hearing stories about them.

"Well," said Aeysha, "my mum and her sister, Hema, are tight as anything now. But they didn't speak to each other for almost eighteen months once."

"Why?" asked Georgia. "Did one sister betray the other in some dreadful way?"

"Oh no," said Aeysha cheerfully. "They fell out over a game of Monopoly. Auntie Hema refused to swap Bond Street for all four stations and the get-out-of-jail-free card that my mum was offering her. They didn't speak for ages. It's lucky it wasn't over something more serious or they might still be feuding. There's one part of my family that still isn't talking to another because of a dispute over ownership of a goat in the nineteenth century. No one can remember anything about it but they still don't speak."

Georgia and Olivia stared at her in astonishment. "You are joking, right?" asked Olivia.

Aeysha grinned. "Of course it might be a family myth, but there's probably some truth in it. Grown-ups can be really stupid some times, and these things get out of control." She turned to Georgia. "It's why you should call your dad and tell him that you love him and you know that he loves you even if he is getting married again and having a baby with Leonie."

Georgia looked bashful. "That's what my mum said I should do, too."

"Then what are you waiting for?" asked Aeysha. "Come on," she said to Olivia. "Let's go sit in the bus. It'll be leaving in ten minutes to take us into town for rehearsals. Georgia can ring her dad in peace and quiet, and you can sit next to Auntie Aeysha and she'll solve all your problems for you."

Olivia stood up with a smile, but inside she wished that Aeysha could do just that. There was a gulf between her and Jack, and since Evie's arrival at the Swan Circus, it was getting bigger by the minute.

Chapter Eleven

"So," said Tom down the phone. "How many jugglers does it take to change a light bulb?" Olivia was so engrossed in watching Jack talk to Evie that she didn't really hear what he'd said.

"Liv?" said Tom into the silence. "Are you still there?"

"Eh, yes," said Olivia, her eyes fixed on Jack and Evie. "What was the question?"

"It's not a question, it's a joke, Liv," said Tom patiently.

"Oh," said Olivia, still not really listening.

"How many jugglers does it take to change a light bulb?"

"I don't know," said Olivia, scowling as Evie put her hand on Jack's arm as if she owned him.

"Only one, but you need an awful lot of light bulbs," said Tom. There was complete silence from the other end of the phone. "Liv?" said Tom. "That's supposed to be funny."

"Sorry," said Olivia. "I'm not really listening."

"I got that impression," sighed Tom. "Liv, is everything all right? You just don't sound like yourself at all."

Olivia gave a long, low sigh. "Everything's fine. Sort of."

"Why don't you tell me what's bothering you?" Tom sounded so sympathetic that Olivia longed to tell him everything. But Jack and Evie were now whispering together conspiratorially and she was desperate to know what they were saying.

"I will," said Olivia. "Sometime. But not now, Tom. I've got to go. Sorry."

She closed her phone without even saying goodbye and walked over to her dad. As she came closer, Jack threw back his head and laughed at something that Evie had said, and several of the Swans standing nearby laughed too. Eel's laugh was the loudest of all. *Little traitor!* thought Olivia, somewhat unfairly.

Evie reached out and lightly touched Jack's arm again. The cheek of it! Evie was behaving as if she was Jack's daughter. And Olivia was sick of the way that everyone seemed to think Evie was so marvellous. Even Georgia and Aeysha had taken a shine to the dark-eyed girl who was so nimble and natural on the wire.

"She's so ethereal," enthused Georgia, watching as Evie pranced across the wire, tossing her mane of dark hair like a pretty pony.

"And what am I, then? Some great elephant?" snorted Olivia, meaning it as a joke, but it came out all wrong and sounded like an accusation instead. Georgia went bright pink and said that she hadn't meant that at all but Olivia had gazed at her so stonily that she gave up. In truth, Olivia did think that Georgia was being disloyal. You were supposed to stick by your friends and stand up for them, close ranks if necessary against outsiders like Evie.

Not for the first time, Olivia wished Tom were there. He'd understand how she felt, she was sure. She wouldn't even need to tell him; he'd just notice. It was all too hard to explain on the phone. But everybody, even Eel, seemed to be welcoming the interloper into the Swan Circus with open arms. Not only had Jack announced that Evie was a better tightrope walker than she was but he'd been delighted to discover that her older sister, Tatiana, was an excellent contortionist who could pack herself away into a small suitcase and put her legs behind her ears.

Olivia had heard him and Pablo talking excitedly about the sisters.

"This is going to make all the difference to *Enchantment*," said Jack. "Evie and Tati will bring variety and real skill that the show was badly lacking," said Jack. "I've been worried all along that we were just faking it, faking it rather well, but faking it nonetheless..."

Olivia stalked away, unable to bear to listen to any more. So she missed Alicia's arrival and what she had to say.

"Yes, it's good to have more talent on board," Pablo had replied to Jack, turning to watch Evie clowning around on the wire and making the Swans laugh. "Even if Little Miss Evie treats wire-walking like a clever party trick."

"Jack, I hope your excitement at having new talent won't make you neglect the old," said Alicia. "I saw Livy's face when you praised Evie so extravagantly in front of everyone the other day. She looked as if you'd just run her over and then reversed back over her body."

"Oh, come on, Alicia, Liv knows how much I rate her!" said Jack defensively. He hated it when Alicia tried to interfere with anything to do with his daughters. But in his heart he knew that she had a point. Liv had seemed so moody since they had been in Edinburgh; and he had been so busy and stressed he hadn't given it much thought. It was as if something in their relationship had shifted. He thought back over the last week and realised that sometimes when Liv looked at him, it felt as if she was judging him in some way. *Perhaps she was just growing up?* thought Jack. After all, she had just turned thirteen. But it felt like something more, as if she were growing away from him, and it made him sad. He had to try and reconnect with her again, but he had so much on his plate he felt quite overwhelmed.

The most pressing thing was a rehearsal to try and integrate Evie and Tati into *Enchantment*, but he also needed to do something to try and get his money back. So far the police had entirely failed to come up with any leads. If they couldn't snare the scammer, he would have to do it himself. Funds were running desperately low, and the last thing he wanted was to have to ask Alicia for a loan. His pride just wouldn't allow it.

Chapter Twelve

The Swans had performed two shows that day, and they were all looking forward to having a free evening for once, their first since arriving in Edinburgh. They were back at the campsite for an evening of games and a supper cooked by Lydia. Evie and Tati had been invited to join them and spend the night, as the Swans had a spare tent. They'd seemed delighted to be asked, and had disappeared from the big top as soon as the second show was over, saying they needed to pick up a few things. They were gone for ages, and everyone was getting tired of waiting for them when they arrived back just before six o'clock, breathless, agitated and full of apologies, with a small tatty rucksack each. As soon as they arrived at the campsite they both asked shyly if they could take a shower.

"Of course you can," said Lydia kindly. "I only wish you could persuade William Todd to have one. That boy seems to be allergic to water." The sisters had disappeared and emerged shortly afterwards, their hair freshly washed. Evie was wearing her distinctive yellow dress with the blue trim.

"Do you want to play rounders?" asked Will. "You can be in my team, as long as we can have Harry as well."

Tati screwed up her nose, but Evie took her sister by the hand and pulled her towards the game. Olivia, who was kneeling down unseen beside her tent doing up her trainers, heard her say: "Come on, Tati, show willing. We want them to like us and trust us, remember?"

"You're one to talk, Evie. You've been so rude to Livy. You even booed her!"

"We got off on the wrong foot at that magic show, that's all," said Evie, a little stiffly. "But the important thing is that Jack and the grown-ups like us. They're the ones who will be able to help and protect us. Olivia doesn't know that I booed her, and I never would have done it if I'd thought at the time what a good cover the Swan

Circus would be for us. I'd have been nicer than apple pie and even licked her shoes for her."

"I think she's rather lovely, and she's talented, too," said Tati. "You've got a lot in common. Maybe you could still be friends?"

Evie sniffed. "She's all right, I s'pose, and maybe in other circumstances we might have been friends. But it's obvious she can't stand me, so we should just stay out of her way and play the sympathy card as much as we can with everyone else."

"Oh, Evie," said Tati, suddenly tearful. "Maybe we should just tell them the truth? They're nice people. Even that scary Miss Swan. I'm sure they would help us."

"We've already agreed, it's too risky," said Evie fiercely. "Come on, stop crying, and let's go and play."

After they'd gone, Olivia stood up, a puzzled expression on her face. Why was Evie so keen for the Swans to trust her and what did she mean about the Swan Circus being a good cover? Why did they need help?

Olivia joined Georgia and Aeysha sitting under a tree eating strawberry laces. They watched the rounders game for a bit. Will's team was winning by miles because Harry kept on making spectacular catches. Evie was pretty good too, running out Kylie Morris with a casual swagger that brought admiring glances and cheers.

"Not just great on the high wire," said Aeysha, "but also pretty good at rounders, too. Is there no end to that girl's talents!"

"If she's so great, what's she doing living in a garage?" asked Olivia shortly.

Aeysha looked at her. "Are you quite certain about what you saw in the garage?" she asked cautiously.

"Certain," said Olivia. She watched Evie run to home base to the cheers of the others. "I don't trust those Purcarete sisters. Why are they trying to worm their way into the Swan Circus? What do they want?"

"I'm not sure they want anything," laughed Aeysha. "They are circus people, it's not surprising that they were attracted to a circus. It must be like home from home for them." She gazed hard at Olivia. "I don't want to upset you, Livy, but are you sure you're not just a little bit jealous of Evie? It would be natural if you were. You've never had any competition at the Swan.

The rest of us, we're used to being surrounded by other kids who are as good or better than we are. We measure our talent against other people's every day. But you don't, and then this strange girl waltzes in and suddenly you've got a rival. I know I would probably be madly jealous in your shoes. Particularly as Jack does seem very impressed with her."

Olivia bristled. With her usual clarity, plain-talking Aeysha had touched a raw nerve and it hurt. Olivia didn't want to be seen as a jealous person.

"Of course not," she said hotly. 'Why would I be jealous of Evie Purcarete? She's rude and she's a show-off. But I don't trust her. It's just too much of a coincidence, her and her sister turning up at the Swan Circus."

"You've got to admit, Aeysha, that Livy has a point there," said Georgia. "Don't you think it's fishy that they are living in the garage where 13 Jekyll Street should be and where we should have been staying, and then they turn up at the Swan Circus, too?"

Aeysha sighed. "Coincidences do happen. I just think that you shouldn't assume they're untrustworthy when you have no evidence."

"But there's more," said Olivia triumphantly. "I overheard them talking about someone called Mitch, and Mitch is the name of the man who swindled Jack! That can't be just a coincidence, surely?"

"Oooh, that does sound odd," said Georgia. "There's definitely something mysterious going on. We should investigate."

"Actually, Livy," said Aeysha, very seriously, "if you really think Evie and Tati know something about the scam, then you should tell Jack immediately." She stood up. "I've got to go and help Lydia with the cooking now, but we should talk about this more later. It's important."

Olivia bit her lip as she watched Aeysha walk away. She knew that her friend was right. She'd had every intention of telling Jack what she'd overheard as soon as possible after the circus-skills workshop, but then after Evie's display and what Jack had said about her prowess at walking the wire, she had felt so hurt and angry that she'd been avoiding her father as much as she could.

"Aeysha's right, you know. You should tell Jack," said Georgia tentatively.

"I will tell him," said Olivia slowly. "But

130

I want to wait until I've got some evidence. Otherwise he might just think I'm jeaous of Evie, too, and I'm trying to get her into trouble. If I have proof, he'll realise that he should never have been taken in by her in the first place and be grateful that I was the only one who saw through her." She looked at Georgia. "You can help me. We should keep our eyes and ears open for any more clues; do a bit of investigating if we get the chance."

"Like real detectives!" said Georgia excitedly.

"Exactly," said Olivia.

"Count me in," said Georgia, with a grin.

A good while later, everyone was sitting chatting and chilling out around the campfire. They had just finished a supper of jacket potatoes cooked in the campfire embers, which Lydia had served with grated cheese, tuna mayonnaise and a big green salad.

"Does anyone want more apricot tart? There's still a couple of pieces left," she asked. "Tati? Evie?" The girls shook their heads and their damp, heavy hair swished. They had already had two pieces each. Jack noticed that they had both eaten ravenously, as if they hadn't had a good meal for days. He was pleased that he and Alicia had invited them back to the campsite for supper.

The Swans didn't really need a campfire, the weather was still balmy, but there was something so magical about gathering around it as dusk fell. Only Pablo and Alicia were absent. They had left immediately after supper. Pablo was driving Alicia back to her B&B because she wasn't feeling well. Her arthritis was really bad, and Olivia knew from past experience that her gran might be confined to bed for the next few days.

The Swans were all eager to find out more about Evie and Tati. Initially, the girls seemed quite reluctant to say much and they had to really push them to open up, but after some prompting they started to talk about their dad and what had happened after he'd died.

"Mum, Evie and I stayed with our aunt Zsa Zsa in Romania for a while, but then she got an animal-training job with a touring circus and left to travel across Europe, and Mum said it was time we moved on too. She had never really settled in Romania and there was nothing to keep us there," said Tati. "We joined a circus too, but then Mum got sick. She was tired all the time. She couldn't do her contortionist act any more."

"I think she knew something was seriously wrong," said Evie fiercely. "She knew she had to think about Tati and me if the worst happened. So we left the circus and came to Scotland, where she'd grown up."

"Wouldn't the circus have looked after you and Tati, even if your mum couldn't work?" said Olivia.

"Not the kind of circus we were with. They were commercial ventures, not the family-run outfit like your dad's, Livy. That old way of circus life is dying out," said Tati.

Jack nodded sadly. "That's true. Lots of circuses are now big businesses, not a way of life. Artists get contracted for a season or two and then they move on to the next job."

"What happened when you came back?" asked Aeysha.

"We didn't have much money," said Tati. "We moved around for a bit. We were in the Highlands for a while in a commune. That's where Evie got Harry, when he was just a puppy. Then we went to Aberdeen for a bit, then Glasgow. Mum was getting worse and that's when she brought us here to Edinburgh, where she had lived as a girl. Her parents died in a fire when she was little and Mum was sent to live with her aunt, Rhona, in a little flat in Morningside."

When Tati mentioned the fire, Olivia nudged Georgia and whispered, "See, I was right! There is a solid connection between them and 13 Jekyll Street. Cora must have been the little girl who survived the fire that woman with the poodle told Dad and me about."

Evie and Tati were so bound up with their story that they didn't notice Olivia whispering. "Mum always said that Aunt Rhona was kind but she didn't understand children as she'd never had any of her own," continued Tati. "She packed Mum off to boarding school as soon as she could. She and Mum had just about kept in touch over the years, but it wasn't a close relationship. But Mum was desperate and hoped Aunt Rhona would help us."

"Only it turned out that Aunt Rhona had died just a couple of weeks before we arrived in Edinburgh," said Evie. "Which was awful for her but awful for us, too. So we stayed in a horrid fleapit B&B. The money was running out. Mum was getting worse by the day; a few weeks later she had to go into hospital. I think she knew she'd never come out again."

There was a short, charged silence, and then the Swans started murmuring how sorry they were. Aeysha squeezed Tati's hand.

"You poor things. Who's been looking after you?" asked Eel, with wide-eyed sympathy.

Olivia noticed that Evie shot her sister a warning glance, and quickly said, "We don't need looking after. Tati is eighteen. She is grown up." Tati said nothing. She didn't look grown up, thought Olivia. Certainly not eighteen.

"But surely you must have some relatives to stay with, however distant?" insisted Aeysha, thinking of her own large clan.

A strange look crossed Evie's face and then she said neutrally, "We have an uncle."

Olivia shot Georgia a look. So the man in the graveyard had been telling the truth! He *was* the girls' uncle.

"Oh, you are lucky," said Eel. "I haven't got any aunts or uncles."

"Come on, Swans," said Jack hastily, as if

changing the subject. "Lydia and I need some help clearing up."

"Actually," said Evie, "it would be good if Tati and I could camp with you all for a while. It would be more convenient for everyone now we are part of the Swan Circus, and you have a spare tent."

Olivia glanced at Georgia again and then she said loudly, "We're only camping because some despicable person took all Dad's money and didn't come up with the house he'd promised to rent to us. It was an Internet fraud." Olivia looked directly at Evie as she said this.

"Oh! It was yo—" said Tati, putting her hand to her mouth in surprise and shock. She glanced at her sister and Olivia saw Evie shift her foot against Tati's leg as if to silence her.

"Oh, Jack, what a terrible thing to happen," said Evie smoothly, but Olivia was certain she detected something guilty in her manner.

"Anyway, why on earth would you want to camp when you've got your uncle's nice warm house to stay in?" Olivia said it so sharply that Jack looked at her, surprised.

"Evie, Tati," he said, "you're more than welcome to stay with us at the campsite. But you need to get your uncle's permission. Perhaps I should ring him? Camping's not very comfortable and it can get rather cold at night, but we'd love to have you stay with us, wouldn't we, Swans?"

Everyone nodded.

"It would be brilliant!" said Eel. "Emmy and I are planning a midnight feast on Thursday night."

"I didn't hear that," said Jack.

"Me neither," said Lydia with a smile.

"Ace!" said Evie. She turned to Jack. "My uncle will be happy for us to stay with you; he'll be pleased to have us off his hands." She glanced at Olivia, looking at her from under her eyelashes with what Olivia interpreted as a look of triumph.

At that moment, Pablo arrived back. "What took you so long?" Jack asked him.

"I got caught up in a police operation. Caused a big traffic jam," said Pablo. "Apparently, there was another one of these robberies this afternoon, but the jewel thieves got away." He looked hard at all the Swans, a smile twitching on his lips. "I hope everyone can account for where they were around five o'clock this afternoon?"

Everyone laughed, but Tati blurted out: "It was nothing to do with us…" She turned beetroot-red and tailed off. Everyone looked at her, a little surprised by her over-reaction.

Pablo laughed. "I was only joking, Tati, don't panic! Ooh, apricot tart! I'll have those last slices if no one else wants them…"

Later, when Olivia, Georgia and Aeysha were lying in their sleeping bags in their tent, Olivia suddenly piped up: "Didn't you think it was odd how Tati reacted when Pablo mentioned the robbery?"

Aeysha sighed. "She just didn't realise it was a joke. It's obvious that Evie and Tati aren't jewel thieves. They're just a couple of kids."

"They were gone all afternoon, too," said Georgia excitedly.

"Remember the sapphires Evie had at the boy's magic show? Where did she get them from?" asked Olivia. "If they're connected with the housing scam, maybe Evie and Tati have got connections with the criminal underworld too?"

"Oh, come on, Livy!" cried Aeysha. "We don't know that they've got anything to do with the scam. The fact they're living in the garages isn't proof. And if you really want to know about the sapphires, why don't you just ask them? I'm sure they've got nothing to hide."

"But what about the Mitch coincidence?" pressed Georgia.

"It's just that, a coincidence! Look," said Aeysha wearily, "if you two want to cook up some kind of mystery, don't mind me. Go ahead. But don't say I didn't warn you. And," at this point she propped herself up on her elbow and looked hard at Olivia, "maybe you should think about why you're so eager to prove that Evie and Tati are not to be trusted."

Olivia blushed. She felt annoyed with Aeysha, but also a bit ashamed of herself. She had never been the kind of person to hold a grudge but Evie just seemed to rub her up the wrong way.

"We just want to get to the truth, don't we, Georgia?" she said defensively.

But Georgia hated any kind of disagreement between the friends and she swiftly changed the subject.

Chapter Thirteen

Eel tugged at Olivia's sleeve. "Look!" she squealed in delight. "It's the White Rabbit. Let's follow him." The Swans were at a promenade version of *Alice in Wonderland*, one of the hottest shows at the Fringe. The show's director, Allegra Featherstone, was a former pupil of Alicia's and had offered the Swans free tickets.

It was unlike any show they had ever seen before. For a start, there was no stage and no auditorium with seats in neat rows. Instead the show was taking place in an old warehouse and the audience was free to wander around all four floors. There was a room where the Mad Hatter's tea party was taking place, another where a caterpillar sat on a toadstool smoking a hookah, and an entire space lined with tiny bottles full of jewelled liquids. Each of the bottles were labelled "Drink Me" and if you were brave enough to do so you were ushered into a hall of mirrors that reflected back big and small versions of yourself.

There was another room laid out like a nursery with lots of cots, and in each of these was a little swaddled felt piglet in a baby's bonnet with a dummy stuffed in its mouth. As they wandered around the building they kept getting distant glimpses of Alices of differing sizes or an angry, red-faced cook with a rolling pin. At one point, they turned down a corridor and came face to face with a projected image of a giant striped cat that kept disappearing from the screen until only its smile was visible.

"It's the Cheshire Cat!" said Aeysha delightedly.

It was a totally magical and topsy-turvy ninety minutes. "It's as if we really have fallen down a rabbit hole into Wonderland," sighed Georgia, her eyes shining with excitement.

"It's like being in a completely parallel universe," said Aeysha. "I can't believe that outside there's a real Edinburgh. This feels realer than real. Sitting in a normal theatre is going to seem so dull after this."

"Not if there's dancing," said Eel solemnly. "Dancing is never dull."

"Gran said it's called immersive theatre," said Olivia. "She told me that Allegra Featherstone was always an oddball even when she was at the Swan. She once staged *The Little Mermaid* in the bath in Alicia's flat for an audience of two at a time, and she transformed that little cupboard in the girls' cloakroom into a jewelled cave for her version of *Aladdin*."

"I've heard Sebastian Shaw talk about that in class," said Georgia. "He said that for years after there were rumours that some people went into the cupboard and never came out again."

"I'm going to check inside when we get back to school," said Eel seriously.

"I think he was probably joking, Eel," said Aeysha, with a smile. The White Rabbit suddenly appeared again, scurrying along the corridor, looking worried and murmuring: "I'm late, I'm late." He started herding them towards another room and on the way they were passed by a furtive Knave of Spades carrying a plate of jam tarts. He offered them to the children. As they licked the jam from the pastry, the girls found a room that had been laid out like a croquet lawn. A game was underway. Georgia waved at Will and Connor, who were over on the other side of the lawn, and Olivia found herself standing next to Evie and Tati.

The game of croquet continued until a murderous glint stole into the Queen of Hearts' eye and she started to swing her croquet mallet around, crying, "Off with their heads! Off with their heads!" The audience began to scatter as she advanced towards them. Aeysha and Eel were carried in one direction by the crowd and Olivia, Georgia, Evie and Tati were pushed towards a small gold door they hadn't seen before. Olivia wanted to try and find Eel and Aeysha, but when she looked over her shoulder she saw the Queen bearing down on them, swinging her flamingo-topped croquet mallet menacingly.

"Come on," she shouted to Georgia, and they followed Evie and Tati through the door and slammed it shut behind them. They all stood in a gloomy corridor looking at each other with scared, sparkling eyes. They knew it was just a performance and that the Queen was an actor – one Georgia was sure she'd seen playing the mother in a stage version of *The Railway Children* – but they were swept up by the delicious terror of the whole thing.

"Phew, that was a narrow escape," said Georgia. She looked along the gloomy corridor, where a single light flickered at the far end. "Shall we go down there?" Tati glanced nervously into the gloom.

"Let's wait until the Queen's gone, and then go back through the croquet room and see if we can find Aeysha and Eel," said Olivia.

Evie's phone bleeped. Olivia was quite tempted to say that it was rude to have your mobile on during a show, but she bit her lip. Evie took the phone from her pocket and as she did so Olivia caught a fleeting glimpse of the sapphires. Evie turned away from Olivia's gaze, flipping open the phone as she did so. The light from the screen shed an eerie greenish light in the gloom. At that moment the door was flung open and the Queen stood illuminated in a dull red light.

"Off with their heads!" she shouted, brandishing her croquet mallet at them. The children screamed and fled, and in her panic, Evie dropped her phone. She tried to pick it up, but the others pushed her forward in their hurry to get away. Olivia scooped up the open phone and set off after the others with the Queen on her heels. Up ahead, the corridor forked in two, and Evie and Tati peeled off to the right while Olivia pushed Georgia to the left. They ran on down another corridor and emerged breathless into a room full of white rose trees, where men were busy painting the roses red.

There was no sound of feet behind the girls. They leaned against the wall, their hearts beating fast, and tried to get their breath back.

"That was a narrow escape," said Georgia. "I feel as if my heart is going to burst."

"Me, too," said Olivia. She glanced at the open phone in her hand. The text message was visible on the screen. Olivia knew she shouldn't read it, but she couldn't stop herself. It said: *You clever, thieving little hussy. What a thing to do to your poor old uncle! Will do deal on the sapphires. Meet me in St Giles' Cathedral 5 p.m. today. Third pew from the front. No tricks. Will make it worth your while. Mitch.*

Olivia gasped. She showed the message to Georgia, who looked shocked. "So you were right, Livy. Evie does know someone called

Mitch and the sapphires are clearly stolen. She must have taken them from her uncle. So that's why he's looking for her."

"Yes," said Olivia. "And she must have told this Mitch person that she's nicked them. It sounds like he's going to buy them from her."

"We have to tell the grown-ups," said Georgia, looking scared. "This is getting really serious."

Olivia shook her head slowly. "Not yet. We still need proper proof. We've got to be absolutely certain."

"So what are we going to do, Livy?"

"We're going to the cathedral and watch to see what happens." Olivia felt a thrill run down her spine.

Georgia looked a bit worried. "We'd have to be really careful not to be seen," she said. "It all seems a bit scary to me."

"It'll be fine," said Olivia. "There are plenty of places to hide in a cathedral."

"Maybe I could get a picture of Evie and Tati with this Mitch bloke on my phone?" said Georgia excitedly. "And then we could show it to Jack and he'd know what the scammer looks like."

Olivia nodded enthusiastically. "That's a great idea." She scrolled down Evie's phone to see if there were any more messages but there was nothing. Then she clicked on the picture gallery and quickly looked through the photos. It made her feel guilty to be looking in somebody else's private photo gallery, but she needed as much evidence as she could find.

There were some pictures of Evie and Tati together and some of a woman who Olivia guessed must be Cora. The woman was laughing in the photograph and with a pang Olivia realised that this woman with the dancing eyes was now dead. She clicked on some more recent pictures as Georgia craned to look over Olivia's shoulder. The pictures were all of the same man wearing a hat angled low over his face. The pictures were often taken from slightly odd angles so his face was never entirely visible, as if the photo had been snapped without him knowing. The date and the time of each photo were recorded in the bottom right-hand corner, and they all seemed to have been taken in hotels. In one, the man was sitting in a lobby reading a newspaper. In another he was entering a lift; in a third he was in a corridor with doors leading off it. In a fourth he was making his way down a fire escape.

"That's Evie and Tati's uncle, isn't it?" said Georgia.

"It is," said Olivia excitedly. "But what odd photos."

"Yes, they're not exactly pics you'd want to put in your album," agreed Georgia.

At that moment the White Rabbit ran into the room and beckoned them to follow him. They were directed into a large room in which the entire audience and cast had assembled for the trial scene. Olivia saw Evie and Tati whispering agitatedly to each other at the back of the crowd. She sidled over and held out Evie's phone to her.

"You dropped this," she said gruffly.

"Oh, what a relief," said Evie. "Thanks ever so."

"We thought it was lost for ever, or that it'd be crushed in the stampede," said Tati.

"It's fine," said Georgia.

"It was really kind of you to pick it up, Livy, I'm really grateful." Evie's dark eyes showed she meant what she said.

Olivia shrugged. "I hate to be without my phone. You never know when you're going to get an important message or need to take a photo," she said innocently. Evie threw her a suspicious look as she turned away.

When they got out of the show Olivia had a text from Tom. *Will be travelling to Edinburgh with Aeysha's folks. So many of us we've had to book almost an entire carriage. Very excited and can't wait to see you all! T xxx*

Me too, texted back Olivia. *We've just been to see some immersive theatre. It was sick.*

Sounds a bit damp to me, texted Tom. *Did you have to wear swimming costumes?*

Not that kind of immersive, idiot, texted Olivia. She felt much more cheerful now that the investigation seemed to be getting somewhere.

Later that afternoon, Olivia and Georgia walked up the Royal Mile towards St Giles' Cathedral. They had slipped away from the group of Swans who were handing out flyers for the next performance.

"Georgie and I are going to try a bit further up," Olivia had said casually.

"I saw Evie and Tati head that way, they should have it covered," said Aeysha.

"Oh well, it's still best if we spread out,"

said Olivia. "You stay here with the little ones."

She and Georgia pushed their way through the crowds who were watching the Fringe acts perform in the late-afternoon sunshine. People kept trying to thrust flyers for shows into their hands. They had put their own flyers in Georgia's bag.

"Come and see *Macbeth* performed on a bouncy castle!" entreated a young man.

"Four-star reviews for a puppet version of *Oedipus Rex*. Described as 'blindingly good' by the *Guardian*," said a woman, waving a leaflet under their noses.

Olivia and Georgia smiled and shook their heads politely. They knew how soul destroying it was to try and sell your show every day, and they had total sympathy for the desperate performers. They had almost reached the cathedral when Olivia spotted the boy-magician. She was irresistibly drawn towards him, even though Georgia pointed at her watch and said it was nearly five.

"Let's just stop a minute," said Olivia. "We need to wait until Evie, Tati and Mitch are there, otherwise they might spot us. We can creep up behind them and maybe then we'll be able to hear what they say."

There was a dense throng gathered around the boy, so they stood on a bench. Even so, they were just able to see him over the heads of the crowd. The boy was in the middle of a complicated card trick but he noticed Olivia and Georgia and gave them a wink. His resemblance to Jack was so astonishing that Olivia felt faint. She knew that her dad had laughed when she'd asked him if he had any other children, but how did she know he was telling the truth?

Olivia grasped Georgia's sleeve. She felt a terrible urge to confide her fear that this boy must be her dad's secret son. What other explanation could there possibly be? She needed to talk to someone about it.

"Georgie," she said, "I know you're going to think I'm insane, but that boy... That boy, I think he could be..."

Olivia stopped. She felt that if she said it out loud she might make it true. Georgia looked quizzically at her, waiting for her to continue. Olivia was very pale and looked so anxious that Georgia felt worried for her friend.

"Are you all right, Livy?" she asked, when at that moment the cathedral bell started to sound. It was five o'clock.

"It's nothing," mumbled Olivia. "I'm just being silly. Forget I said anything." She took a deep breath and jumped down from the bench. "Quick, Georgie, we've got to go to the cathedral or we'll miss Evie, Tati and the mysterious Mitch."

But they already had. As Olivia and Georgia entered the cathedral, a very tall, thin man and his small, squat friend pushed roughly past them and out of the door. The interior of the cathedral was cool and dark, and after the bright sunshine outside their eyes took a while to adjust.

When the two girls got near the front of the nave, they could see that although there was a smattering of people in some of the other pews, there was nobody in the third pew from the front. A woman was righting a wooden plinth and candle that looked as if they had been knocked over. She was muttering "kids" under her breath as she did so, and she eyed them suspiciously.

"We're too late," said Georgia disappointedly. "I knew we shouldn't have stopped for the magic show!" They went out through the side door that led into the crypt café but they could see no sign of Evie and Tati.

"Let's go back to the others," said Olivia, and they headed back down the Royal Mile. They spotted their friends a little way away and were walking towards them when they noticed the man they had seen in Greyfriars Kirkyard loitering as if he were keeping an eye out for someone.

As they walked past he caught Olivia's eye and smiled in recognition.

"Hello again," he said. "I'm still looking for my niece. I'm worried she could be in trouble, her and her sister, poor wee bairns." He sounded really distressed. "I just want to help them. I feel I've let them down."

Olivia and Georgia looked at each other. They wondered whether they should tell him that they actually knew Evie and Tati, and that his nieces were mixed up with a criminal called Mitch. Perhaps they should mention the sapphires?

"Well…" said Georgia uncertainly, but she got no further because Aeysha came running up.

"There you are! Where've you been?" Aeysha didn't wait for an answer. "Just hurry

up, will you, we're going to be late for the show."
She looked quizzically at the man, then cast an exasperated glance at Olivia and Georgia and started dragging them away.

As they hurried down the road she said tartly, "I know from the way you two are always whispering together that you're up to something. I've noticed and I reckon Evie has, too. I just hope you know what you're doing and I hope you didn't tell that man that Evie and Tati are staying with us?"

"But, Aeysha, he's their uncle, the one they mentioned. We're sure of it," said Georgia plaintively.

"That's what *he* says," said Aeysha, and then she added darkly: "And that's what Abanazer told Aladdin so he could get the jewels. I wish you would just let Evie and Tati be. They've never done anything to harm either of you."

"Do you know where they are?" asked Olivia stonily.

"Yes," said Aeysha. "I saw them come rushing out of the cathedral about ten minutes ago, and I don't think they'd been leaving the vicar a flyer."

Chapter Fourteen

Jack had added some new routines to *Enchantment* since Evie and Tati's arrival at the Swan Circus and he was putting everyone through their paces in a rehearsal. Olivia and Evie were up on the wire, moving towards each other slowly and watchfully. Both were wearing long robes with cowls over their heads so they looked slightly sinister as they glided towards each other. The pair of them stopped some distance apart, dropped their cloaks to the floor many metres below, and stood facing each other in glittering leotards and tights. Evie was dressed entirely in white and Olivia in black.

Watching from below, Aeysha thought how much they reminded her of two cowboys squaring up to each other in one of those old westerns that her dad loved so much. It wasn't surprising really: inspired by the final scenes of *Hamlet*, Jack had come up with the idea of a carefully choreographed duel high up on the wire. Both the girls were holding balancing rods that they used as staves to attack and defend themselves. Pablo had managed to spotlight them really dramatically and Kasha had written some brooding music that built to a crescendo as the fight reached its climax.

From down below, the performance was powerfully compelling, but up on the wire, things were rather tense. Olivia and Evie were testing each other every step of the way. Jack had choreographed the fight sequence with great care and impressed upon each of the girls that they had to follow his instructions to the letter. He wasn't taking any chances and he didn't want any accidents. He had insisted that both wore safety harnesses, although Evie had loudly protested that she hadn't needed a harness since she was four and the Magnificent Purcarete would never have made her wear such a thing. Olivia bit her tongue. The unkind thought, *And look where recklessness got him*, crossed her mind and she felt ashamed of herself. It was just that she hated the way everyone bent over backwards for Evie and Tati, and seemed to put up with such a lot from them.

"Let's try that again, girls," called Jack. The music began, and Olivia and Evie moved across the wire towards each other again. Olivia had to admit that Evie was skilful and admired the way she moved so gracefully, but she also thought she was flashy and attention-seeking. How could Jack possibly think Evie was so good, when she walked the wire with a flamboyance of a kind that he'd always said he'd detested? Evie used the wire as a place to show off and play to the crowd, and it was certainly working with the Swans, thought Olivia crossly, who were behaving as if they had never seen anyone walk it before. It made her feel very small, and unimportant.

But at least the routines she did with Jack were the backbone of the show. Evie may have wormed her way into the Swan Circus but she couldn't take her double act with her dad away from her.

Evie was approaching her with a glint in her eye. There was the satisfying clunk of wood on wood and the two girls leaned into each other with their staves in a cross formation. They both counted silently to three then broke apart, and as she did so, Evie gave a little double twirl that was totally not in the sequence.

Olivia waited for Jack to stop them and tell Evie off, but to her disgust, he shouted: "That was great, Evie. Do you think you could manage it, Liv? Not to worry if it's too difficult for you."

Olivia felt rage rise in her stomach. Manage it? Of course she could manage it. If her dad wanted her to behave like a little show-off, that's what she'd do. The green snake curled ever tighter in her stomach.

The two girls faced each other again. Evie danced towards Olivia, an infuriatingly superior little smile playing on her lips. Olivia scowled at her. She wanted to wipe the smile off Evie's smug face. Never in her life had she wanted so much to slap someone, but she knew she'd never do something so awful and embarrassing. Instead, she clenched her fists. Evie did another twirl that wasn't in the routine.

"More!" shouted Jack from below. Olivia obeyed. The two girls whirled apart along the wire and then whirled back again like human spinning tops. They came closer and closer. For a split second Olivia felt tempted to whirl into Evie and send the two of them spinning off the wire, but such a deliberate act of sabotage was beyond her. It went against everything that Jack had ever taught her.

The girls came to a whirling stop just centimetres from each other. They raised their staves again and there was another clunk as the two sticks met. They could feel each other's weight. Their eyes locked. They were so close that Olivia could feel Evie's hot breath on her cheek.

"Not bad for a beginner," said Evie, with a patronising smirk.

Olivia felt as if a volcano had erupted in the core of her stomach and hot fury was trying to force its way up through her body and out of her burning throat. But when they came, Olivia's words were a quiet snarl. "I know about you," she said.

Evie suddenly became very alert, like a bird sitting in the low branch of a tree that had suddenly sensed a cat prowling within striking distance.

The two girls broke apart. "You don't know anything about me," hissed Evie as they came together again, their staves hitting with real force, but there was a trace of something fearful in her defiance.

"Oh yes, I do," said Olivia quietly, as she stalked Evie, who was walking backwards. "I know lots of things. I know that you're not living with your uncle. I know that you've been camping out in a garage in Jekyll Street. And I know that your uncle's looking for you."

Evie gave a little mewl of surprise but she didn't miss a step in the sequence.

Enjoying herself, Olivia continued. "I know all about the jewels and I know all about the house scam," she said softly in Evie's ear. "Maybe it's time I called the police?"

Evie took an agitated step backwards, looking at Olivia with anxious eyes. She had turned so pale that her freckles stood out on the bridge of her nose. She attempted a twirl but as she did so, she lost her footing and plunged off the wire.

Olivia looked down at Evie dangling helplessly in her safety harness and flailing around like an overgrown baby. The wire was bouncing up and down but Olivia kept her balance. She remembered Evie's boastful words on the day of the workshop: *I never fall*.

She saw a small tear fall down the cheek of Evie's upturned face. On the ground below, Harry set up a howling that sounded as if his doggy heart was broken.

When Evie had lost her footing, Olivia had – for the merest split second – felt a surge of triumph. But now, looking down at her humiliated rival, she felt only guilt and misery. She might just as well have pushed Evie off the wire. Instead of feeling jubilant, she had never felt more ashamed of herself in her whole life. She felt even worse when they were back on the ground and all the Swans gathered around Evie, asking if she was all right after her fall. Olivia hung back and hoped no one noticed how guilty she looked.

Chapter Fifteen

Olivia sat at a table in a café picking at a baked potato. She wasn't hungry. She could see Harry lying patiently outside, his head on his front paws, waiting for Evie. That dog loved Evie; he would die for her. Aeysha was right, thought Olivia, if Evie could inspire such loyalty in Harry, she couldn't be all bad.

Sitting opposite Olivia were Eel and Emmy. They were planning their future careers as prima ballerinas, and getting annoyed with Kylie, who was telling them that to be a classical dancer, you had to go to the Royal Ballet School.

"The Swan's great for acting and musical theatre," Kylie was saying knowingly, "but if you want to be a professional ballerina, then the Royal Ballet School is the place to be. My little sister is starting there in September. You can go to White Lodge in Richmond Park when you're eleven. It's the best."

"But I never want to leave the Swan and Gran," said Eel worriedly.

"I don't want to leave the Swan, either," said Emmy, looking tearful.

"Well," said Kylie, "you can't want to be a ballet dancer enough."

"But I do!" said Eel indignantly. "I want it mostest. Although I do like tap and modern, too, and I loved that contemporary dance show that Gran took us to see at The Place. It's just that I could never leave the Swan."

"Perhaps you're just not prima ballerina material, then," said Kylie, nodding gravely.

Eel and Emmy looked at each other in horror.

"Oh, shut up, Kylie, for goodness' sake! They're only eight, they don't have to worry about all this for ages," Olivia had snapped with such uncharacteristic rudeness that the others looked at her in surprise. Kylie flushed bright red and went off to sit at another table in a huff.

"Are you all right, Livy?" asked Eel, a worried frown on her face.

"I'm fine," said Olivia brusquely. But she didn't feel fine at all. She needed someone to talk to and she wished again that Tom was there. She looked longingly over at the other table where Georgia and Aeysha were sitting with Evie and Tati. They were all laughing uproariously at a story Evie was telling.

Olivia looked away. When they'd all arrived at the café, Georgia and Aeysha had bagged a table with four chairs in the far corner. Olivia was at the back of the group and was fighting her way through the crowded café towards them when Evie had slipped into one of the empty seats and Tati into the other. Olivia thought she saw Evie throw a little glance of triumph in her direction, but maybe she had imagined it.

Olivia was full of conflicting feelings about Evie. She still resented Evie for the way she had so easily wormed her way into the Swan Circus, but she felt intensely guilty when she remembered her forlorn, frightened little face when she had fallen off the wire. But, thought Olivia to herself, her shot in the dark about the necklace and the scam had clearly hit home. Evie was not to be trusted.

"Olivia! Olivia!" Lydia's voice woke her

from her reverie. She looked up and realised that everyone else was heading for the door.

"Come on, Livy." Georgia's mum smiled. "We need to get a move on. I'll be in terrible trouble if I get you all back late for the afternoon performance." They set off towards Calton Hill, with Olivia striding ahead. She came to a small road and waited for everyone to catch up before she crossed and began texting Tom.

As the others joined her, Olivia found herself standing next to Tati. Evie was just behind them. Olivia and Tatiana stepped out into the road, with Olivia just a little in front. She wasn't taking much notice because Tom had just texted her back. Suddenly, Harry started barking frantically as a blue car came careering around the corner at high speed.

The Swans scattered like skittles. Olivia heard Tati scream as the car bore down on them and then she felt a hard yank that pulled her backwards. She couldn't keep her balance and fell heavily on her left arm, while the car roared over the spot where she had just been standing. Aeysha and Georgia rushed to pick Olivia up.

"Are you OK?" they cried as they helped their friend to her feet.

"I'm fine," said Olivia. "I've just hurt my arm a bit." But she was shaking so much that she could hardly get the words out.

Tati was crying and trembling, too, and was being talked to fiercely by a white-faced Evie, who kept throwing anxious looks in Olivia's direction. Olivia heard her say the words, "It's a warning." Eel and Emmy were in tears as well.

Olivia kept insisting that she'd just bruised her arm in the fall. But by the time they got to the big top, it was clear that Olivia's arm was much worse than that.

Jack heard them arrive and appeared from inside the tent. "Here at last!" he said impatiently. "We've only got forty minutes before show time…" He stopped when he saw their shocked faces and Olivia cradling her arm protectively. "What happened, chick?" he asked, hugging his daughter, his face full of concern.

Olivia suddenly realised that she didn't really know. It had all happened so fast. There had been the speeding car and then somebody had pulled her backwards and she had fallen and hurt her arm. She caught Evie staring at her very intently. There was something almost challenging in Evie's look, as if she was very interested to hear what Olivia was going to tell her father. Olivia was certain it was Evie who had made her fall on her arm. But had Evie yanked her to save her from the speeding car? Or was it revenge for what had happened on the wire? What had Evie meant by "It's a warning"? Was the accident her way of telling Olivia to back off?

She opened her mouth to speak, but Eel was already telling Jack about the car. "Thank goodness Evie knocked Livy out the way or she could have been run over. Evie's a real hero."

There were loud murmurs of agreement from the other Swans. Olivia felt more confused than ever. She lifted her head and her eyes met Evie's. Evie looked away quickly as if embarrassed. Tati's face was taut and anxious.

"We're going to have to get you to the hospital, Liv, chick," said Jack. "I want that arm checked out. It doesn't look like it's broken, but we can't take any chances."

"But what about the show?" asked Kylie.

"I'll take Livy to the hospital," said Lydia. "You stay here, Jack, and get the show up with Pablo. We'll probably be hours in A&E."

"But we can't do the show without Livy!"

wailed Aeysha.

"I'll just have to walk the wire on my own," said Jack. He looked worried. "But it's a bit of a disaster, because we've got a reviewer from the *Scotsman* and some bloggers coming in this afternoon. The show just won't be the same without you, Liv, but nobody can fill in for you."

"If it would help, I could take Olivia's place," said a quiet voice. "I pretty well know the routine. Of course, I can't do the trapeze, but I can do the double act with you, Jack."

Everyone turned to look at Evie and began babbling enthusiastically. Olivia suddenly felt completely invisible. She desperately wanted Jack to say that it was very kind of Evie to offer but nobody could possibly take his daughter's place, but she could see from his anguished face that this wasn't going to happen. He was torn between wanting to give the best performance possible for the critics and knowing how upset Olivia would feel being replaced.

"We need to ask Liv if she feels comfortable with that," he said anxiously. Olivia felt everybody's eyes on her. She swallowed hard. Jack had left her no choice.

"Of course Evie must do it," she whispered.

When Jack came to hug her as the taxi arrived to take her and Georgia's mum to the hospital, he whispered how proud he was of her, but she closed her eyes and turned away from his embrace.

Chapter Sixteen

"There's a brilliant review in the *Scotsman*!" shouted Aeysha. "Five stars! Look!"

There were whoops of delight as she waved the page that included a big picture of the Swans in the silks sequence. The Swans had been busy warming up for the lunchtime show but at Aeysha's words they'd all stopped what they were doing and crowded round. Aeysha began to read the review out loud. She glanced apologetically at Olivia as she read out: "*The highlight of the show is undoubtedly the tightrope* Tempest *scene with Prospero and his daughter, Miranda, which was played out with thrilling grace by the famed high-wire walker, Jack Marvell, and the astonishing thirteen-year-old Evie Purcarete, a real circus star of the future.*"

The others cheered delightedly, and Olivia put on a bright, fixed smile so that nobody would see how much it hurt. She stiffened when Jack put a discreet but sympathetic arm around her and whispered that reviewers often didn't really know anything about the circus. She looked at Evie, expecting her to look horribly smug at the glowing review. But in fact she looked really worried, and Olivia heard her anxiously asking Pablo how the critic had known her name. Pablo explained that they'd given him a special sheet detailing each segment of the show and listing all the performers' names.

Evie chewed her bottom lip and went rather quiet. A few minutes later, while the other Swans were all still poring over the review and dissecting every detail, she sought out Jack, who was standing with Eel while she rang Alicia with the good news about the review. Olivia had kept her distance to avoid having to speak to her grandmother and therefore bursting into tears, but when she saw Evie go over to Jack she moved in closer.

"But how can you be sure it's safe?" Evie was asking, her dark eyes full of anxiety.

"Well, I can't be completely certain, of

course," said Jack. "I was worried about the big top myself at the start. Thought it might be a target for vandals. But it's been fine so far, so I've no reason to think it won't be in the future." He peered closely at her anxious face. "What's suddenly brought this on, Evie?" he asked kindly.

Evie shook her head. "Nothing. I just wondered."

"Well, don't worry about it," said Jack, with a smile. "If somebody wanted to get into the big top at night I guess it would be relatively easy. But who on earth would want to do harm to a circus?" He patted her on the shoulder as Eel handed him the phone.

Olivia didn't move.

"I can think of someone," she heard Evie mutter grimly to Tati.

Tati's eyes widened anxiously. "You think he might see your name in the paper and come here to find us? Oh, I'd never forgive myself if…" She put her hand over her mouth as she realised that Olivia was listening. The two sisters moved away.

Olivia watched them go, thoughtfully. It sounded as if Evie and Tati were mixed up with some pretty nasty people.

The excitement over the review refused to die down. Kylie Morris was reading the best bits out loud for at least the fourth time to the Swans' delight. Olivia was so afraid that the others would see tears glistening in her eyes that she said she had to go and help Georgia's mum. She didn't want her friends to feel sorry for her, so she made herself scarce until the show began and she didn't even reply when Eel sent her a text saying, *Are u all right? Dad worried u might be upset. PS Evie is no way as good as u, all of us think so.*

Olivia finished counting the money in the cash box, locked it and dragged her feet towards the big top. The show had been on for over twenty minutes and she couldn't expect any more latecomers. It was quite a good house. More than 150 people, many of them families whose children had attended the circus-skills workshop that morning. The numbers were an improvement but still not enough to break even. She could tell from Jack's tense face how worried he was about money. Maybe the review would make all the difference?

Olivia shivered as she crossed the grass,

the first big drops of rain plopping on her head from a dark, threatening sky. The brilliant spell of good weather, so unusual during an Edinburgh August, was clearly breaking with a vengeance. She shifted her arm in its sling. It wasn't broken. Just badly bruised. At the hospital they'd said she should rest it but she would soon be right as rain. It was a funny expression, thought Olivia, because rain was seldom right, unless perhaps you lived in a desert.

The weather fitted her mood. Lightning flashed above the castle as Olivia dipped inside the tent. She handed the cash box to Georgia's mum and settled herself in the darkness in a seat right at the back of the ring. When the interval came she would be expected to help serve drinks and snacks to the audience. She could feel the audience like an animal in the dark. An audience might be made up of many individuals, but somehow when they came together in a theatre or big top they seemed like one big, powerful creature.

It should be me up there, thought Olivia fiercely as Kasha's music swelled and Jack and Evie stepped on to the wire. She could hardly bear to watch them. Since she'd been tiny, she'd dreamed of doing a double act with her dad and now Evie had usurped her. She thought how often she, Aeysha and Georgia said, "I'm so jealous," when one or the other of them had got a fabulous new pair of shoes or something, but of course she had always been really pleased for the other person's good fortune. But she didn't feel like that about Evie. Her bad luck had been Evie's lucky break. If it had been bad luck? Maybe Evie had pushed her deliberately?

The crowd broke into applause as Jack lifted Evie effortlessly on to his shoulders and the girl stood there proudly without even the hint of a wobble. A boy a few feet in front of Olivia said very loudly: "That girl is brilliant, Mum, isn't she? Do you think that man's her dad?" Olivia's eyes glazed with tears and she fled the big top, running blindly across the car park before banging straight into someone who was also hurrying away from the circus.

"You!" said Olivia, forgetting to apologise to the boy-magician in her surprise. "What are you doing here again?"

The boy blushed, and pushed back his unruly hair. He looked more like a young version of Jack than ever. "How do you know that I've been before?" he asked.

"I spotted you in the crowd when I was up on the high wire," said Olivia.

"I just really wanted to see it again." The boy looked dreamy. "It's so magical. It makes me feel as if someone has cast a spell over me."

"Then why are you leaving so early?" asked Olivia. "We haven't even got to the interval yet."

The boy looked embarrassed. "I'm supposed to be at home. I slipped out without permission. I'm going to get into big trouble. And anyway, it's not the same without you. I can see that girl's very good, but I don't feel the same when I watch her. When you were on the wire I felt as if I was up there with you." Olivia's heart gave a little skip. He glanced at her hurt arm. "Is that why she's doing it instead?"

Olivia nodded. "I had an accident," she said, before adding darkly: "If it *was* an accident."

The boy was wide-eyed. "Don't you believe it was?"

"I don't know what to believe any more," said Olivia in a small voice.

"Is that why you're crying?" The boy's likeness to Jack and his directness unnerved Olivia, but she smiled and nodded. The boy might be a good couple of years younger than her, but he was so easy to talk to. She felt as if she had known him all her life.

"That, and because I'm so jealous of Evie being up there with my dad." From the tent they could hear the music reach the crescendo that marked the end of the double act, followed by a brief silence and then rapturous applause. "I feel...I feel as if she's pushed me out like a cuckoo pushes an egg out of a nest."

"You don't look like an egg," said the boy with a smile. "You're much too pretty to be an egg." He sighed. "It must be amazing to share something like high-wire walking with your dad." Olivia's stomach tightened. She wanted to ask about the boy's father, but she was also desperately afraid of what she might find out. What if he *was* Jack's son? It would make her feel as if they had all somehow been living a lie, that they weren't the family she had thought they were. She'd never be able to trust her dad again.

"You said the other day that you aren't allowed to go to the circus," said Olivia. "Why is that?"

The boy shrugged. His phone bleeped and

then immediately started to ring, but he ignored it. "I don't know. My family are just really against it." His phone bleeped urgently again.

"Do you live in Edinburgh?" asked Olivia.

"Yes," said the boy. "I live in one of those big houses in Stockbridge. You could come visit if you like, if you get time off from the circus." His phone bleeped furiously again.

Olivia took a deep breath. She was desperate to ask more questions, but she didn't want to frighten him away. "Do you have any brothers and sisters?"

"I'm an only child, worse luck. I don't even have cousins," said the boy. He smiled. "If I had a sister, I'd want her to be like you."

Olivia felt on the verge of blurting out her suspicions. As casually as she could, she asked: "What about your mum and dad?"

"My mum died," said the boy. Olivia's stomach lurched again. "You do ask a lot of questions," he said. His phone bleeped, then began to ring. He looked at it and frowned. "I'm sorry, but I have to dash."

He set off at a run. Olivia realised that she hadn't asked him the obvious question. She sprinted after him. "Your name! What's your name?" she called.

The boy didn't stop, but he shouted back over his shoulder: "It's Alfie. Alfie Marvell."

Olivia's legs suddenly gave way. She uttered a little mewl of pain and crouched on the grass holding her stomach. Her phone began to ring. She noticed that the call was from Tom, but she still pressed ignore.

Chapter Seventeen

Olivia walked out of the toilet block with her washbag under her arm, and passed the campsite's little shop with its closed sign. It was a few days after her conversation with Alfie and the weather had turned really nasty. She was busy struggling to open her umbrella when she realised that there was somebody talking in the old red telephone box by the shop. The windows were all steamed up so whoever was inside couldn't see out and she couldn't see in. The door wasn't quite closed and Olivia was certain it was Evie's voice she could hear. She wondered why she was using the old-fashioned telephone box when she had a perfectly good mobile phone.

"Tonight. The Imperial Hotel. Be there."

Olivia heard the clunk of the receiver being replaced, and drew back into the shadows. The door of the telephone box opened and Evie and Tati emerged, looking furtively around.

"What if they can trace the phone call?" asked Tati.

"I wasn't on long enough," said Evie.

They set off towards their tent. Olivia waited a few minutes until they'd disappeared inside and then she put up her umbrella and plodded across the field to her own tent. The rain had eased a little, but the sky was heavy with thick, black clouds and from far away came a growl of thunder. The wind was whipping up too, so Olivia had to angle her umbrella carefully to stop it blowing inside out. As a result a rivulet of rain was running down her forehead and on to her nose, where it dripped mournfully off the end.

Olivia was looking forward to the warmth of the tent, which was glowing cosily, but as she came nearer, she heard Eel's voice. What she was saying brought Olivia up short.

"I think Livy's really unhappy about something." Her sister's voice sounded sad. "Dad's really worried about her. He thinks she's avoiding him."

Then Aeysha said: "Well, she *is* behaving very weirdly."

Olivia quietly clicked off her torch and stood frozen to the spot. They were talking about her! She knew no good ever came of eavesdropping, but she couldn't help herself. It was becoming a bit of a habit.

"It feels a bit like when she fell out with you two and Tom over *The Sound of Music*," said Eel.

"It does," said Georgia, "but in that case Katie Wilkes-Cox was being a witch and stirring things without any of us knowing. So what we thought was happening and what actually was happening were two quite different things."

"I spoke to Tom earlier," said Aeysha. "He's worried, too. He said that she's not returning his calls."

"What can we do?" Georgia's voice came next. "Livy is convinced that Evie and Tati have something to do with the scam and the man who swindled Jack out of his money."

"Well, what do you think, Georgia?" asked Aeysha. "You're the one who's been going around with her like you're in some spy novel."

Olivia guessed that Georgia was blushing at this. "I don't know. Some of Evie and Tati's behaviour *is* a bit suspicious."

"Are you sure that Livy isn't just jealous of Evie?" asked Aeysha. "I think there's something more, something we don't know about. Something is gnawing away at her. I can't put my finger on it, but I have a feeling it goes right back to the day the others arrived here in Edinburgh."

"I think it might have something to do with that magician boy," said Georgia excitedly. "Livy started to say something about him the other day but she didn't finish."

"Maybe you could ask her about it?" said Aeysha.

"I dunno," said Georgia. "Since the accident she's almost stopped talking to me too. I wish Tom was here. He'd get through to her, and find out what's going on."

Outside the tent, Olivia shuddered as water ran off the umbrella and down the back of her pyjama neck. It roused her. Since she had learned Alfie's name, she'd felt more and more disconnected from her friends, the other Swans, the circus, even from Eel. Everyone was behaving as if the world still turned in the same way, but for her it didn't. It had changed. Her arm was much better, and Jack had suggested that she rehearse with him tomorrow and maybe even take part in the evening performance. But she didn't want to. She couldn't bear the thought of being up on the wire with him, the two of them putting their complete trust in each other, trust that was built on a lie.

Olivia sighed. She wished that her gran was around. But Alicia was still suffering badly with her arthritis and Olivia didn't want to bother her with the stuff about Jack. She was just going to have to have it out with her dad. Tell him that she knew about Alfie and that he couldn't keep it a secret any longer. He'd have to come clean.

Right, she thought, and coughed loudly to let the others know that she was coming in. Silence fell in the tent. She stumbled inside, smiling brightly, and began pulling off her wellington boots.

Everyone turned to beam at her and began talking at once.

"There you are, Livy!" said Aeysha, a little too brightly.

"Hello, stranger, where've you been?" said

Georgia, a little too loudly.

"Cleaning my teeth," said Olivia shortly.

"Lydia says that Will Todd's teeth are going to drop out. She's convinced they haven't seen toothpaste since the day he arrived," said Aeysha.

"Yes," said Georgia, "he's driving Mum to distraction."

"Maybe that should be *extraction*," said Aeysha, with a grin. Georgia shrieked with laughter, and even Eel got the joke. But Olivia just sighed.

There was an awkward silence, and then Eel said: "I'd better get back to my own tent. Emmy and the others will be sending out a search party." She stuck her head outside. "It's starting to blow a gale," she said. "See you in the morning." She looked back at her sister and said very solemnly: "I love you, Livy. Loads and loads."

"We all do," said Aeysha, quietly reaching for her friend's hand.

Olivia knew she was going to cry but fortunately everyone called goodnight to Eel and Aeysha turned off the torch. The three of them lay in the dark.

"It's great you're going to be able to go back on the wire tomorrow," said Aeysha into the darkness.

Olivia knew that Aeysha was being kind and trying to be a good friend, but she felt so fragile she could hardly speak. She longed to confide in her friends and tell them why she was angry with Jack and mistrustful of Evie, but she knew that if she did she would break down completely, so she just said gruffly: "I'm tired," and rolled over with her back to the others.

She lay staring into the darkness for what seemed like hours, until she could hear the steady breathing of the others. The rain was lashing down and the wind tore at the canvas as if it had claws. She heard a party of Scouts, who were camping further down the field, pass by on their way back to their tents, laughing and joking. For a while it was quiet, apart from the rain hitting the tent like tiny stones and the howl of the rising wind. Then she sensed movement outside and heard two men talking in low voices. She listened harder and realised it was her dad and Pablo.

"Are you sure this is a good idea, Jack?" asked Pablo.

"Anything that gets me my money back is a good idea," whispered Jack fiercely. "We're really low on funds, Pablo. Things are desperate. I know audiences are picking up very nicely, but it's not enough. This may be nothing, but it's a lead and it's worth following."

Their whispers faded away, and a minute or two later Olivia heard a door slam and the bus's distinctive engine start up. It lumbered along the rutted track that led to the road. Olivia's heart was beating faster. She hoped they would both be safe, particularly on such a filthy night.

Then Olivia heard another noise outside the tent. More people were passing by, despite the rain. Somebody tripped over the edge of the tent, and Olivia heard Evie say something rude before Tati shushed her. Aeysha stirred in her sleep, coughed, turned over and fell back into a deep slumber.

Olivia sat up. Where were Evie and Tati going at this time of night? They were heading for the road. She remembered what she'd heard Evie saying on the phone – they must be going to meet someone at the Imperial Hotel that night!

She eased herself out of her sleeping bag,

unzipped the tent as quietly as she could and slipped on her wellies. She crept into the cold air, shivering in her thin pyjamas. At least it had briefly stopped raining, although the sky was ominous and the wind evil. She had her torch in her hand, but she didn't dare turn it on. She kept her distance, worried that Harry would scent her presence.

Evie and Tati were almost at the end of the track. She heard a car coming down the lane and stopping. There was the faint click of doors opening and closing. Olivia hid behind a tree and saw that the car was a taxi that reversed into the track and then turned back towards the city.

There was a sudden flash of lightning followed by a loud clap of thunder. Olivia jumped. She felt frightened: for her dad and Pablo, and for herself standing under the trees when a storm was coming. She ran back to the tent and clambered inside just as more rain began to fall, coming so thick and fast it was as if somebody had trained a machine gun at the canvas. The wind had whipped itself up into a frenzy. Olivia was amazed that the others could sleep through such a racket.

She lay awake, listening to the storm. The

walls of the tent felt so thin and insubstantial. She wished she was in her nice warm bedroom back at the Swan where she felt safe and protected; she wished they had never come to Edinburgh. The wind caught the front of the tent and it began to flap wildly where she hadn't quite secured it properly. Aeysha woke up and groaned, then there was another flash of lighting immediately followed thunder so loud that it made Georgia sit up and scream.

"What's happening?" asked Aeysha. There was a note of panic in her voice.

"It's all right," said Olivia, on her knees trying to secure the flapping canvas. "It's just a really bad storm. I'm sure we're safe." But as she said the words there was a strange roaring sound, followed by a bright flash and terrible rumble, and the entire tent seemed to lift off the ground. Olivia fell back on top of Aeysha and the three girls clutched each other in terror, screeching in alarm. They heard a terrible tearing sound as if a mad-axe murderer was hacking at the canvas, and a gaping hole appeared in the side of the tent. The wind came screeching like a banshee through the hole and whisked the tent away as though it were made of tissue paper.

The girls found themselves sitting in the middle of the field, the torn tent in tatters and the rain battering down on them.

A strange sight met their eyes. The mini-hurricane had blown a path right through the part of the campsite where the Swans had pitched their tents, but the rest of the campsite was virtually untouched, the tents still intact, if a little battered. The Swans were in complete disarray. Several of their tents were in shreds while Connor and Will's had disappeared entirely. Somehow, Will was still fast asleep in his sleeping bag, snoring gently, and blissfully oblivious to the rain and all the people running around him trying to retrieve their scattered belongings.

Lydia was trying to gather everyone together and simultaneously comfort Emmy, whose teddy bear, Mr Bossyboots, had been blown into a prickly bush and couldn't be retrieved. Connor shook Will, who sat up and looked around him with a dazed expression. "Where am I?" he kept saying, as if he had awoken to find himself on the moon.

"Where are Jack and Pablo?" Lydia was asking. "We need the keys to the bus; we can take shelter there while we dry off and work out what to do."

"They've gone off somewhere in it," said Olivia shortly.

"What?" Lydia shook her head in irritation. "Well, they should have said where they were going," she said sharply, reaching for her phone. There was no answer from either Jack or Pablo's phone, so she left Pablo a curt message. "Georgie and Livy, help me herd everyone into the toilet block out of the rain and then we can count heads and check nobody is hurt."

Several other campers had staggered out of their tents and were trying to help. One of the Scout leaders fetched Mr Bossyboots from the bush, while Olivia and the others ushered the younger children towards the toilet block. At least the wind had died down now, as if it had worn itself out with all the huffing and puffing, and the rain had turned to a steady drizzle.

It seemed astonishing that just a few minutes before the weather had wreaked such total devastation, then returned to normal so quickly. Everyone was soaked through and miserable, and Eel was shaking with cold and crying because she couldn't find her favourite tap shoes.

"I'll go look for them," said Olivia, giving her a hug. "But really, Eel, if all you've lost are your tap shoes, you should count yourself lucky. Kylie's clothes are halfway up a tree. If the storm had been any worse we might have lost our lives."

She could hear Lydia on the phone talking urgently to someone who she guessed was Alicia. She tramped across the field using her torch to pick a path through the devastation, and occasionally stopping to pick up an item of lost clothing. She discovered somebody's drenched iPod and Georgia's favourite green skirt that her dad had bought for her in a vintage shop on a day trip to Brighton.

Olivia shivered. Her feet were wet because her wellies had blown away and she was wearing flip flops. At least it had at last stopped raining, although the trees were still dripping furiously. She tried calling Jack. There was still no response. She hoped that he and Pablo were safe. She found the wreckage of Emmy and Eel's tent, pulled it apart and quickly found Eel's missing tap shoes. She turned back towards the toilet block and as she did so she discovered a small wooden box half hidden under the side of a nearby collapsed tent. She picked up the box and some of its contents spilled out. On the lid were engraved the initials E. P. – Evie Purcarete!

Olivia picked up the computer print-outs and newspaper clippings that had fallen out of the box. She carefully unfolded one of the newspaper clippings. It was a bit damp and fragile but perfectly readable.

Jewel Thief Strikes Again, read the headline above a report about the series of rooftop raids on Edinburgh hotels that had been puzzling the police all summer. Olivia shuffled through the clippings. They all referred to the robberies. Why on earth would Evie be keeping these news reports unless she was involved in some way? Maybe her own uncle wasn't the only person she'd stolen from? Evie certainly had the skills to clamber across Edinburgh's roofs in the dead of night. Maybe that's what she was doing at this very moment. Maybe she was robbing the Imperial Hotel!

Olivia glanced at one of the computer print-outs. It took her a second to realise that it was an advertisement for a house available for rent in Edinburgh during the Festival. The very same non-existent house that Jack had paid for! Olivia's heart skipped a beat. Finally she had evidence directly linking Evie to the scam.

She rifled through the papers, which turned out to be all of the e-mails between Jack and Mitch. Only someone who had access to Mitch's e-mail address could have these. Olivia felt sick. What was Evie up to? What did she want? Was it another swindle? Whatever it was, she wasn't going to let Evie Purcarete get away with it.

Chapter Eighteen

Olivia sat in the back of the minibus, holding her sister's hand, as they drove towards Edinburgh. She was trying to comfort Eel and Emmy. Eel was upset that nobody knew where Jack was, and Emmy, clutching a sodden Mr Bossyboots, was missing her mum and wanted to go home. They'd had to hire two minibuses and a taxi to get into town, and now they were driving through the dark deserted streets in the dead of night. Everyone was unnaturally quiet. It was as if they were all suffering from delayed shock at what had happened and the realisation that they had had a very lucky escape.

Nobody said anything but many were wondering if their Edinburgh summer was over for good. The minibus driver had the local radio station on low and they could hear ongoing reports of the freak storm. Every time there was a gust of wind Emmy squealed, and Eel had decided that the reason they couldn't get through to Jack was because a tree had fallen on the bus, trapping her dad and Pablo inside.

As soon as Alicia had turned up in a taxi at the campsite, she had taken control. She gathered everyone together and that's when they realised that Evie and Tati were missing. Lydia had put her hand to her mouth in horror and said, "I completely forgot about them. I was just counting Swans. Goodness, what can have happened to them? You don't think they could be with Jack and Pablo, do you? Maybe we should call the police."

Several of the children began to cry, but Olivia said, "Evie and Tati know how to look after themselves. I saw them leave the campsite in a taxi around midnight."

Alicia looked relieved, before observing grimly that half the circus were running around in the middle of the night. "I'll be having stern words with Evie and Tati when we find them," she said. She looked hard at the Swans. "You do realise that if any of you slipped away like that, you'd be straight on the train back to London and your parents, and facing a very uncertain future at the Swan." Everyone nodded with serious faces and chattering teeth.

"Right," said Alicia, "we need to get you all somewhere warm and dry, and since Jack isn't here to make any decisions, he'll have to live with mine." Olivia and Eel knew from the set of Alicia's mouth that Jack was in big trouble.

Their grandmother stepped outside and was soon talking quietly and urgently on her mobile. Shortly afterwards, the minibuses turned up and they all piled in, clutching what remained of their possessions.

Alicia asked the drivers to put their heaters on full blast, and soon the Swans grew so warm and toasty that several of them dozed off. Not Olivia. Her mind was racing. Where were her dad and Pablo? Were they in trouble, and what would they think if they turned up at the campsite and found the smashed tents and the Swans gone? She wanted to ask Alicia where they were going so that she could text Jack and let him know where to find them, but there was something about the grim line of Alicia's mouth that made her reluctant to speak to her grandmother. In any case, Alicia seemed to be doing a great deal of texting herself in her rather laborious fashion that made Olivia want to snatch the phone out of her gran's hands and do it for her. Alicia found texting particularly difficult because of her arthritis, so Olivia guessed that if that was what she was doing, it was because she didn't want her conversation overheard. She sent another text asking Jack to call her urgently.

The little convoy of vehicles rumbled over the New Town cobbles. Olivia thought she glimpsed the street where Kasha's aunt had her flat and wondered if that was where they were all heading, but she wasn't surprised when they kept on going – she'd paid the boys a visit with Georgia and Aeysha, and the flat was tiny, smaller even than the B&B where Alicia was staying. Maybe they were going to a hotel, although she wasn't sure what kind of hotel would welcome the Swans in the middle of the night looking like drowned rats.

The minibus turned into a street full of cafés and delis, continued a short way through an area with a village feel, turned down another street and stopped outside a large house with black railings, wide steps and a big front door with a large lion's head knocker. Everyone climbed out of the buses and taxis, and stood sleepy and subdued in the street while Alicia paid off the taxi-drivers from a wad of cash, walked up the steps and knocked gently on the door.

The door opened immediately, as though someone had been waiting for them. They walked into an entrance hall so large that it easily contained a sofa, several chairs and a large bookcase. A staircase curved elegantly into the hall from above, and Olivia could see it spiralling up at least three floors to a domed atrium. It was the grandest house she'd ever been inside.

"Through there are flasks of hot chocolate, coffee and sandwiches, and blankets all ready for you," said the man who'd opened the door, indicating a room off the hall, where a fire could be seen crackling in a huge fireplace. The Swans, shooed along by Lydia, sleepwalked into the room, but Olivia hung back in the hall, holding Eel's hand. She saw Alicia and the man kiss each other on the cheek and murmur something to each other, and then the man moved away from behind the door, which he hadn't quite closed properly, and for the first time she could see him quite clearly. He was in his mid-thirties and very good-looking in a dark, brooding way. He looked so familiar she wondered if he was an actor she'd seen on TV or on the stage.

"So," he said with a smile, turning his attention to the girls, "you must be Olivia and Eel. Alicia has told me so much about you both. I'm Michael." He was about to speak again when there was the clatter of feet on the stairs and a small figure appeared, then stopped abruptly halfway down. Olivia and the boy-magician stared at each other in amazement.

"You! The high-wire girl!" said the boy, his eyes round with astonishment. "What are you doing here in the middle of the night?"

"Alfie!" breathed Olivia, but it came out as a froggy croak. So she had been right all along! If Alicia had brought them to this house, then she must know that Jack was Alfie's dad! It all fitted together like the pieces of a jigsaw. Michael and Alicia looked surprised.

"You two know each other?" asked Michael uncertainly. Alfie nodded.

Olivia felt a little hot coal of fury and misery flare into life in her stomach. "Oh yes," she said sarcastically, "we know each other. Although I don't think anybody has ever bothered to introduce us." The anger was running like molten lava through her whole body, making her both rude and recklessly brave. Her face was burning with fury. She stuck out her hand very formally towards Alfie as he walked down the stairs, a puzzled expression on his face. He looked at her hand warily.

"Hello, Alfie Marvell," she said. "I'm Olivia Marvell. What nobody has bothered to tell you, and they certainly haven't bothered to tell me, is that we're related–"

There was a sudden hammering at the door. It burst open, almost knocking over Alicia. A wild-eyed Jack barged into the hall just as Olivia announced: "–and you and I, Alfie, we're half-brother and sister. Your dad is my dad…"

There was an appalled silence as the adults all looked at each other. Eel's mouth dropped open and she said indignantly: "Nobody told me I had a brother! Even half a one. What's going on?"

Alfie looked totally bemused. He kept shaking his head and looking questioningly from the grown-ups to Olivia and back again.

"Liv…" said Jack urgently, reaching out for her. Olivia took a step away from him and backed into her grandmother's arms. Alicia held her protectively.

"Keep away," Olivia snarled.

Jack looked as if she'd struck him. "Oh, Liv, chick, I'm so, so sorry. I've made a real mess of things," said Jack. "Liv, please, it's not what you think, I promise…" He tried to give Olivia a hug, but she pushed him away very hard. He looked desperate. "Alfie isn't your brother, Liv, he's your cousin."

Olivia looked at her father in bafflement. "Cousin? How can I have a cousin when I haven't got any uncles or aunts?" she demanded.

"Because you do have an uncle. Me." Michael put out his hand to Olivia and said: "Jack's my wayward little brother. I'm very pleased to meet you, Olivia. I've always wondered what Jack and Toni's daughters would be like, and now I know." He paused and a wistful look came into his eyes. "You look just like your mother, Olivia. She was a beautiful woman."

Olivia noticed that Alicia's eyes were

shining with tears. "But I don't understand," she spluttered. She turned indignantly to Jack. "You're always keeping secrets from us! Why didn't you tell us you had a brother, and that Eel and I had an uncle? And a cousin."

Jack looked anguished. "Because Michael and I fell out a long time before you were born and we haven't spoken since. Not for years."

"Why did you fall out?" asked Olivia, determined to get to the bottom of the secrets. "That day when the Swans arrived in Edinburgh. I heard you say to Gran that you'd done something that was a betrayal, something of which you were really ashamed."

Jack closed his eyes for a second as if experiencing a sharp pain, then he looked at his brother. He turned to Olivia and said very gently, "You're right, Liv. I did do something very terrible, something that hurt Michael very much indeed."

He glanced at Alicia, who appeared to be holding her breath. "It hurt other people, too."

"What was it?" whispered Olivia. She'd thought she'd wanted to know the truth, but now she was about to get it, she wasn't so sure. The urge to put her hands over her ears was huge, but Jack was already speaking in a low voice.

"Michael…my brother, the brother I loved very much and who I knew loved me because he had always looked out for me since we were boys, was going away for a few days. He asked me to look after the woman he loved, and who he intended to marry, while he was gone. When he got back, Toni and I had run away together. I'm ashamed to admit that I was too much of a coward to face him."

Olivia stared at her uncle. Now she knew what Sebastian Shaw had meant.

"So you were in love with my mum?"

Michael nodded.

"You were going to marry her. You were engaged?"

He nodded again. "It was a very long time ago, Olivia. Soon after Jack and Toni eloped, I met Ginny, Alfie's mum, and I loved her very much, right up to the moment of her death." He looked at his son. "If I'd never met Ginny, Alfie would never have been born, and he's the best thing in my life. Hearts do mend, Olivia, even badly broken ones like mine. I've long got over losing Toni, but I've never got over losing my brother." He gave Jack a long, serious look. "It's good to see you, Jack. I've missed you more than I can say."

"I'm so sorry..." blurted out Jack, but Michael just stepped towards him and enveloped him in a hug.

When they broke apart, after a long time, Jack said, "I think what we all need is a family chat, and Michael and I will tell you everything. No more secrets. Secrets tear families apart."

Eel considered Alfie with a beady bird-like gaze. "I've never wanted a brother, because really one sister, particularly one as moody as Livy, is quite enough," she told him confidentially. "But I know I'm going to *love* having a cousin."

"Good," said Alfie solemnly, but with a twinkle in his eye. "I think I'm going to *love* having cousins, too."

Chapter Nineteen

"When we were boys," said Michael, "Jack and I did everything together. Jack was three years younger than me, but we were more than brothers, we were best friends. We put on shows together in the garden with our friends. But Jack and I were in charge. We did everything ourselves. Writing the scripts, creating the music on an old cassette player, making the scenery. Jack was always very good with his hands. The shows were always rather swashbuckling affairs, and they always had two essential ingredients."

"What were they?" asked Alfie.

Jack, the girls, Michael and his son and Alicia were packed closely together on the two big sofas in the drawing room. Pablo had disappeared to help Lydia settle the rest of the

Swans upstairs in some of the many bedrooms. Georgia and Aeysha were sleeping in a four-poster bed that had room for at least six. But Olivia, Eel and Alfie insisted that they weren't tired and that they wanted to hear what Jack and Michael had to tell them immediately.

"Better out than in," advised Alicia. "We don't want Livy jumping to any more conclusions."

So they had all settled down on the sofas, interrupted only by a text from Evie to Jack saying that she and Tati were safe and were on their way. Michael and Jack talked and talked. They started with their lonely childhood. They had busy parents who had little time for their two sons, who took refuge in each other's company and putting on shows.

"But what were the special ingredients in the shows?" repeated Alfie insistently.

"We each had a speciality," said Jack. "Mine, of course, was acrobatics and later the slack rope and tightrope. I eventually went off to join a circus in Europe when I was barely seventeen. But your dad did magic tricks. He was a really brilliant stage magician."

"Just like you, Alfie!" said Eel.

Alfie turned bright red and looked worried, and Olivia added quickly: "He's amazing. He's got a real talent for it – like father, like son."

Michael was looking intently at his son. Alfie took a deep breath. "I found all this conjuring paraphernalia and books in the attic years ago," he said to his father, "but when I tried to show you my first trick after weeks and weeks of practice, you got really angry and told me to put it all back where I found it and never ever touch it again. But I couldn't let it alone. I've been practising in secret ever since."

"You must have been," said Eel, "because you've got really good." Then she added sagely: "That happens when you practise a lot. It's happening with my dancing."

"Are you angry with me?" asked Alfie, looking at his dad anxiously.

"Oh, Alfie, of course I'm not angry," said Michael. "Just ashamed that I was cross with you when you first found all the conjuring stuff, and tried to stop you from doing something you obviously really love. You clearly have a real talent."

"But why did you get so angry?" asked Olivia, who was increasingly beginning to think that all grown-ups were mad.

"Because it reminded me of a self I thought I'd long buried." He looked at Jack. "Shall I continue?" His brother nodded.

"I first met Toni at a post-show party for a West End production of Shakespeare's *Twelfth Night*. She played Viola."

"Viola's one of my middle names," said Olivia excitedly. "I've read the play. Viola gets shipwrecked with her brother and she thinks he's drowned, but he's not, he's still alive. But she doesn't know that."

"That's right," said Alicia softly, "and Viola dresses up as a boy and the great lady Olivia – who you are also named for – falls in love with her. It's a play about mistaken identities, illusions, deceptions and misunderstandings, about people not seeing what they think they see or only seeing what they want to see." Then she added drily: "A bit like this family, really."

"I'd been employed by the producer to do a magic show to entertain the cast and guests at the last-night party," said Michael. "I was a struggling playwright in London at the time, I'd just had my first play accepted by the Royal Court but not yet produced and I was supplementing my income by doing conjuring shows. That was the night I met Toni. I made her disappear."

"You made our mum disappear!" said Olivia breathlessly.

"Yes," said Michael. "She asked me to." Then he added with a twinkle: "But only after I'd sawn her in half. I noticed Toni at once. Who couldn't? She wasn't just beautiful. She had an aura about her, as if she lived just a little more intensely than anybody else." He smiled. "Maybe a bit like you, Olivia. I'd been to see *Twelfth Night* twice, buying cheap seats right up in the gallery, and like everybody else in the audience I was already a little bit in love with her, or at least with Viola.

"At the party she was like a bright shimmering light attracting everyone towards her, so I was surprised when she suddenly detached herself from a group of famous theatre people and came over to talk to me. After all, I was just the hired help. A nobody. We chatted for a bit and I told her about my play, and then she asked if I could really make people disappear and I laughed and said it was all an illusion, that of course I couldn't really make somebody disappear but I could make people think that I had. Then she said that sometimes all the constant attention made her wish that she could disappear. I remember her saying very clearly: 'Tonight I wish I could be anywhere else but here.' So I said that if she would act as my assistant for the night I would arrange it."

Olivia and Eel were wide-eyed.

"How?" they asked in unison.

Michael glanced at Alfie. "Do you know?" he asked his son.

Alfie nodded. "I found the box for that, too. I've been working on it. I'm not perfect, but I almost managed to make Angus McMillan disappear when he came round for tea, but he got claustrophobic and wouldn't let me do it again after the first time, even when I promised him my school pudding for a whole week."

Michael put his finger against his nose and said to Olivia and Eel. "I can't tell you, it's against the magician's code to give away secrets, isn't it, Alfie?" Alfie grinned and nodded. "So," continued Michael, "I made your mum disappear that night. She walked into the box, and when I opened it a few minutes later she wasn't there. All that was in the box was the costume that she had worn in the play when Viola had dressed up as a boy and called herself Cesario. Everyone was amazed, but I think they all understood that it was her way of saying goodbye to the play and to them. That she was moving on."

"Where had she disappeared to?" asked Eel.

"Only to the pub around the corner," said Michael with a grin, "and I soon joined her there. Before the evening was over I'd fallen in love and six months later we were engaged."

"She was nineteen," said Alicia quietly. "She had the world at her feet. Both of you did. Your play became a massive success. The two of you were going to be the toast of the West End, you both had such glittering careers ahead of you."

"Then what happened?" asked Olivia.

"I came back," said Jack.

Chapter Twenty

A pinky glow in the sky could just be spotted through a crack in the thick curtains. The first birds were beginning to sing. Jack was talking in a voice so low that Olivia and the others had to lean forward to catch his words.

"I'd been in Europe travelling with a couple of circuses since our parents had been killed in a car crash. I missed Michael so much, but I was getting a real education in walking the high-wire, and I didn't have any money, so trips home weren't an option. Then I heard that a circus needed a tightrope walker for a show in London. It was only a three-day gig, but it was a chance to get back to the UK and see Michael. I knew he was engaged to be married. We tried to write to each other, but I was always on the move and it was in the days before mobile phones and an Internet café on every street corner. We hadn't had much contact."

"I was thrilled to see you," said Michael, "but then I had to go to Edinburgh because the Traverse Theatre was about to put on a play of mine. I was starting to do really well, and I was in the middle of writing my first Hollywood screenplay. It meant I wouldn't get a chance to see Jack perform, but I knew that we'd have time together after I got back. He was going to be staying on for a couple of weeks. So I gave him the keys to my rented flat, got Toni two tickets for the circus so she could go and watch him, arranged for them to meet up afterwards, and told him to look after her for me."

"I remember the night Toni and I went to the circus as if it was yesterday," said Alicia, a look of great sadness etched on her face. "Toni was tired. She was in rehearsal at the National. She was going to play Nina in Chekhov's *The Seagull*. I told her we didn't have to go. I was never very keen on the circus, I thought it vulgar and always loathed all those not very funny clowns, but she said it would be rude not to turn up. So we did. For years afterwards I regretted it. She was entranced by everything, but she was most entranced by you, Jack. When you stepped out on the wire, it was as if she was stepping out there with you. I could see it in her face. It was closed and dreamy, and afterwards when everyone else was clapping she sat as if in a daze and she just said four words, and I'll always remember them, because they were so strange and yet so utterly right: 'He inhabits the air'.

"It was as if she was enchanted. I knew at that moment that she was lost to me and Michael, although I did everything I could to stop it. It was like trying to break a spell or to stop a giant boulder rolling down a hill. I tried to make her come back to the Swan with me that night, I even told her my arthritis was playing up, but she wouldn't and in the end we had a terrible row and I stormed off. She didn't come home. Perhaps if I'd stayed, things would have turned out differently."

"I don't think so, Alicia," said Michael. "What was going to happen was going to happen."

"What did happen?" asked Olivia.

"Toni came to find me after the show. As

soon as I saw her, I knew. I knew she knew it, too. The French have a phrase for it. It's called a *coup de foudre*. Being hit by a thunderbolt. Love at first sight."

"Like in *Romeo and Juliet*," breathed Olivia.

"Yes. I felt as if I had suffered an electric shock. My entire body tingled and hurt. All I could think of was that line when Romeo first sees Juliet and he says: '*O, she doth teach the torches to burn bright!*' Of course we fought it. We were very young, still both teenagers, but we weren't complete kids, we knew what we were doing was going to cause pain for a lot of people. For us, too. Neither of us wanted to hurt Michael, we both loved him very much, and I know this sounds like an excuse but it's true: it was stronger than both of us.

"We knew everyone would try to stop us being together, you in particular, Alicia, because you'd think that Toni was throwing away everything, a life of security with Michael and her own glittering career, and that's why we acted like cowards and ran away together, leaving a note in Michael's flat."

"If only you'd told me yourselves, maybe I'd have understood," said Michael quietly.

"I got on a train to Edinburgh to tell you, Michael, but I got off at Berwick-upon-Tweed. I sat on the platform for hours trying to find the courage to get on another train. But I couldn't. I didn't even have the courage to face my own brother and tell him to his face," said Jack bitterly.

"That's what hurt the most," said Michael. "That's why I told you I never wanted to see either of you ever again. And I meant it at the time, although there have been many times I've regretted it since. I wanted to come to Toni's funeral, but Alicia didn't want me to and she was so consumed by grief that I had to respect her wishes."

"I don't blame you for not wanting to see me," said Jack. "It's the one thing in my life that I feel really ashamed about, so ashamed that I couldn't bear to contact you all these years. Not even when I heard that you'd got married, that Alfie had been born and Ginny had died. Can you ever forgive me?"

"Oh, Jack, I already have. I forgave you a long time ago, but I let things simmer. I'm as much to blame as you are. We've both been fools, we should just be grateful that luck and the kids have brought us back together." Michael hugged his brother and then hugged his son.

"It's so strange," breathed Olivia, "to think about your parents when they were young and how they might have loved other people before they loved each other. Might even have married other people."

"Yes," said Alfie, "and just think – if what happened hadn't happened, none of us would ever have been born."

"What a horrible thought!" said Eel. "That would have been a terrible tragedy for the entire world." Everyone laughed.

"Eel Marvell, you have the biggest ego the world has ever known," said Olivia, "and I love you for it. I'm so glad you're my sister. I'm never going to fall out with you, ever."

Suddenly, they heard a dog bark and someone knocked on the door.

"That must be Evie and Tati," said Eel. "They're back."

"Yes," said Olivia, peering out of the curtains, "but the big question is, where have they been?"

Chapter Twenty-One

Alicia went to the front door and Olivia stood up to get a glass of water. Alfie showed her the way to the kitchen and disappeared. She was filling a glass from the tap when Jack came into the room.

"Are you all right, Liv?" he asked. Olivia turned to face her father and nodded. She rested her head against his chest and told him all the things that had happened to make her think that Alfie was his son, and how furious she was with him for keeping secrets from her and Eel.

"I'm so sorry for what I've put you through, chick," her father said, stroking her hair. "I understand why you were so angry with me all this time. Now Michael's forgiven me, I just hope you can, too."

"It was my fault too," Olivia said. "I put two and two together and made five. Actually about a hundred and five." Jack smiled, then Olivia added passionately: "I didn't know what to believe! I was so confused. I thought that if you weren't the person I thought you were, then I couldn't be the person I'd always thought I was."

Jack hugged her closer. "That's the problem with secrets," he said. "They muddle things and set up false trails, then send you off on wild goose chases." He smiled wryly. "A bit like the one Pablo and I went on tonight."

"Where did you go?"

"We thought we had a lead about the house swindle. But it turned out to be a red herring. I'm sorry we weren't there when you and the Swans needed us. I'm such a rubbish dad." Jack pushed his hand through his hair and Olivia saw how defeated he looked. She opened her mouth to protest, but he silenced her. "I'm sorry to say it, chick, but I'm afraid that the Swan Circus is over, the storm has blown away more than just our tents. We probably need to cut our losses and go back to London."

A bark came from the hallway, and they

heard Alicia's raised voice demanding to know where Evie and Tati had been.

"I'm so disappointed with you both," she was saying. "Running around Edinburgh in the middle of the night without telling anybody where you were going! Anything might have happened to you. I know you're not Swans, but while you stay with us you will behave like Swans, or you'll have to go back to your uncle. I'm sure he wouldn't put up with this kind of irresponsible behaviour. Maybe I should have a word with him."

"Oh dear, I better go out there before Alicia eats them alive," said Jack. "And that's another thing, Liv, you really shouldn't feel jealous of Evie."

"But you're always saying how great she is!" cried Olivia, tears springing into her eyes. "You said she was the best high-wire walker of her age that you had ever seen, and we're the same age! That really hurt."

"Oh, Liv," said Jack. "I'm so, so sorry. I may have said that but it wasn't really what I meant at all. If I'm honest, she does have the technical edge over you just at this moment in time, but that's something you'll crack with more practice. But high-wire walking isn't just about technique. It's about heart and soul, and that's what you have and that's what makes you so special. Watching Evie on the wire is like watching a dancer who can execute all the moves perfectly, but who never puts anything of herself into the dance, who does it with cool brilliance but entirely without passion. Watching *you* on the wire is like watching somebody who is risking everything. You give us a glimpse of your heart and soul."

Olivia blushed. "But you always seem to favour her over me," she said softly.

"Maybe I do," said Jack, with a sigh. "But it's because I feel sorry for her and Tati. I haven't wanted to pry, but I'm pretty certain those kids have had a terrible time. They're like a couple of stray dogs. Anything we can do to make their lives better, if just for one summer, is worth doing."

Olivia blushed again, but this time she felt ashamed. Then she remembered the contents of the box. She was worried that Jack was way too trusting of everyone, that's how he had got into trouble in the first place. She reached in her pocket and drew out the computer print-outs of the housing advert and the e-mail exchanges. She handed them to Jack. He puzzled over them for a minute and then it dawned on him what they were. "Where did you get these, Liv?"

She explained about finding the box by Evie and Tati's tent at the campsite and then showed him the initials engraved on it. Then she explained how she was certain there was a connection with 13 Jekyll Street because of what she'd seen of the makeshift hideaway in one of the garages on the day the Swans arrived in Edinburgh, and how she had overheard them talking about a man called Mitch and seen the text from him.

"So," she concluded, "I think Evie and Tati must be connected with the scam in some way."

If Olivia had thought that Jack was going to be excited to have a new lead, she was disappointed. He just looked sad and said: "Poor, poor kids. I reckon it's even worse for them than I thought."

"There's something else—" said Olivia, who wanted to show him the newspaper cuttings about the robberies, but Alicia was calling Jack urgently and the moment was lost.

Olivia and her father walked back towards

the drawing room, and as they passed through the hall, Olivia saw the morning paper lying on the mat. Under the big headline about the freak storm was a smaller headline: *Jewel Thieves Target Imperial Hotel*. An attempt to steal some diamonds from the city's grandest hotel had been thwarted when an anonymous caller had tipped off the police, but despite the stake-out, the thief or thieves had escaped over the roof.

Putting two and two together, Olivia was now certain that she knew exactly where Evie and Tati had been tonight: trying and failing to stage another robbery!

She must tell Jack immediately. She ran into the living room but stopped at the doorway, because Alicia was in full flow.

Evie and Tati were subdued and hollow-eyed. Alicia was still reading them the riot act.

"I know that Tati is eighteen and can do what she likes, and I know that you're both not really our responsibility. But we feel responsible for you. When we discovered you were missing we were really worried. We would have called the police if it wasn't for the fact that Livy had seen you disappear off in a taxi, and we had other things to worry about at just that moment."

At the mention of the police, Evie and Tati looked really uncomfortable.

"We're sorry," said Evie. "But we had something very urgent that we had to do."

"What was it that couldn't possibly wait until morning?" asked Alicia. "I want to know where you have been."

Evie looked pained and Harry went over to Alicia and offered his paw. "You're not going to win me over that easily," she said tartly, adding: "If you don't trust me enough to tell me, why should I trust you?"

Tati looked as if she was going to burst into tears and Evie stuck her lip out defiantly. Jack intervened. "Look, Alicia, the girls are clearly exhausted. I think they've got the message. Why don't I have a chat with them in the morning?"

Evie and Tati looked at him gratefully while Alicia pursed her lips. "Well, see that you do, Jack," she said. "Come, Livy, we need to get you into bed, you look fit to drop. Jack, can you ask Michael to show you where Evie and Tati are going to sleep."

With that, she bundled her granddaughter away upstairs. When Olivia had the chance to creep out of her bedroom half an hour later, she found Jack and Michael deep in conversation together in the drawing room. She'd have to tell her dad about the newspaper another time.

Chapter Twenty-Two

Olivia and Jack were up on the high-wire. Olivia walked towards her father. She felt as if she was floating rather than walking across the wire. He lifted her in one seamless movement on to his shoulders. She stood there triumphant and she didn't wobble at all. She felt safe as houses. She felt as if she had come home after a long time away. She jumped down on to the wire. Jack grinned at her. "Welcome back, partner," he said. Olivia loved this. She didn't want anything to spoil it. Not ever.

Olivia stepped off the wire, gave Jack an ecstatic grin and ran down to the ring below, where the rest of the Swans were gathered with Pablo and Michael. They were all watching Alfie go through his magic routine. Everyone clapped wildly each time Alfie pulled off a really difficult trick.

The Swans were all tired but happy. When they had woken on the morning after the storm, they had been certain that they would all be heading back to London. Last night, quite a number of them had wanted to. Kylie said that she was going to ring her mum first thing in the morning and tell her to come and collect her. She'd had quite enough of Edinburgh, playing to half-empty houses, eating sandwiches and freezing to death in the tents. She didn't relent even when Georgia pointed out that before the storm hit they had been having lots of fun, too.

"I want out. To think I gave up two weeks in the South of France for this," Kylie had said miserably, as she'd crawled into bed. "I want to go home."

But in the morning, she and the other Swans had felt quite differently. The sun was shining and the day promised to be a scorcher. From downstairs came the smell of bacon sizzling and when the Swans had trooped into the kitchen they had found freshly squeezed orange juice, toast and honey, thick creamy porridge with fresh raspberries from the garden, warm Danish pastries and chocolate muffins.

They were soon feeling much more cheerful, and when they heard that Michael had asked them to stay for the rest of the Festival, they realised that they had landed on their feet.

Alfie began a new trick, pushing up his hat again as it slipped over his eyes.

"He's good, isn't he?" said Olivia to Eel, who was standing next to her.

"He is," she replied, "and I'm glad he's our cousin, not our half-brother."

"So am I," said Olivia.

"Alfie's promised to saw me in half," said Eel happily, slipping her hand into her sister's. Since Eel had discovered that Alfie was her cousin, she'd been following him around like a small dog.

"I'm not sure that's something most people would look forward to," laughed Olivia.

"I can't wait. I've always wanted to be in two places at the same time," said Eel solemnly.

"Well, unlike some people, just make sure you let Gran know exactly where you are," said Olivia. Eel's eyes grew round.

"Gran's furious with Evie and Tati, isn't

she? Where were they? Everyone wants to know what they were doing out in the middle of the night."

"So do I," said Olivia quietly.

Everyone cheered again as Alfie drew a rabbit out of a hat and then another and then another. The rabbits were a bit frisky and escaped off the table and started to run about the ring. The children gasped as they saw Harry bounding towards them, his tongue lolling with excitement.

"He's going to eat them," cried Georgia, but Evie just smiled and whistled and Harry started to round the rabbits up as if they were just very small sheep.

"I swear that dog has a brain the size of a computer," said Aeysha, "and you've trained him really well, Evie."

Evie smiled again. "It's what I really want to do, be an animal trainer like my aunt, Zsa Zsa. The high-wire, it's fun, but it was my dad's thing, not my thing. He wanted me to do it, so I did it to please him. But I don't have a passion for it like Livy does," she said. Olivia looked at her stonily.

Evie shrugged and whistled again.

Harry herded the rabbits towards Alfie, who picked them up. "We should put them out in their run so they can have some grass," he said, stroking them affectionately, and Eel and Emmy ran to take them.

"Right," said Michael to his son, "let's see if you can master the disappearing act!"

"That would be mega," said Alfie happily.

"I'm not sure it'll be ready for your Swan Circus debut tonight, but maybe you can premiere it at the end of the week if you really practise hard."

Magic show over, the Swans all drifted away to rehearse. Olivia watched while Jack drew Evie aside and led her up the steep rake of the big top to the highest seats, where they could have a little privacy. She saw Evie's shocked face when he pulled out the print-outs. The two of them talked intently for several minutes, and then she saw them shake hands as if concluding a business deal. A few minutes later they came back and joined the rest of the Swans.

"What happened?" hissed Olivia to Jack. "Did you ask them where they were last night?"

"I didn't get an answer on that, but I did get something more valuable," he said with a grin. "I'm going to get my money back."

Olivia bit her lip. She wanted to tell Jack about her suspicions that Evie was involved in something far more serious than the house swindle, but what if she was wrong? Maybe there was an innocent explanation for everything she had discovered about Evie and Tati? She remembered how in her first term at the Swan she had been accused of stealing when she was entirely innocent, and how terrible it had felt. She had to be certain before she made any accusations. After all, she had already got it badly wrong about Alfie. She was going to keep a very close eye on Evie and she wouldn't say anything until she was quite, quite certain.

"Be careful, Dad," she whispered. "Don't put all your faith in Evie. If she *is* involved in the scam, maybe she isn't to be trusted at all. Maybe, maybe..."

"Spit it out, Liv," said Jack.

"You know those robberies that have been taking place all over Edinburgh..." said Olivia, turning red. She broke off when she saw the incredulous look on Jack's face.

"Liv," he said. "That's pretty serious stuff. Do you have any proof?"

Olivia blushed a deep crimson. "Well," she muttered, "Evie was keeping all these newspaper reports about the burglaries, and whenever the police are mentioned she looks really worried, and her and Tati's disappearances often seem to coincide with when jewels go missing. There was a robbery last night while they were gone and they wouldn't say where they had been and I heard…"

"That's not evidence, that's just putting two and two together and making five," said Jack.

Olivia was ashamed to see a flicker of disappointment in his eyes. "Maybe I'm jumping to conclusions," she murmured, wishing she hadn't said anything.

"Maybe you are," said Jack quietly. "Whatever those two little waifs are, I very much doubt they are international jewel thieves."

To Olivia's relief, Alfie suddenly gave a huge whoop from the other side of the ring. "I've done it, I've really done it!" he cried triumphantly. "I've made my dad disappear!"

The Swans looked around. There was no sign of Michael.

"I saw him walk into the box, but when

Alfie opened the door he wasn't there," said Eel, wonderingly.

"Oh, Alfie, you can do real magic, just like Harry Potter," sighed Emmy.

"Where's he gone?" asked Eel, sounding a bit worried.

"I think you'll find," said Alfie, with the twinkle in his eye that made him look so much like Jack, "that he's gone back to the house to cook spaghetti and homemade tomato sauce for our tea." Everyone laughed.

Olivia sat down to answer a text from Tom asking how things were. She texted back: *Better. Have discovered I have long-lost cousin. He's called Alfie. He does magic.*

Seconds later, Tom texted back two words: *That's wizard!*

Olivia smiled. It was a very Tom thing to say.

Chapter Twenty-Three

The three Swans and Alfie crept through the dark streets of the Old Town. They headed up steep steps and narrow twisting alleys where the ancient buildings on either side leaned together as if too exhausted to stand up straight.

Even though it had gone one o'clock in the morning, there were quite a lot of people around. They passed pubs and bars where they could see people drinking and talking, lit by haloes of light. They passed the open back door of a pub that led directly on to a small stage where a stand-up comic was dying on his feet. His attempts to engage the drunken crowd were being met with jeers and cat-calls. Aeysha thought how horrible that must be, and decided the comic was very brave.

As the children entered a maze of isolated back streets it got quieter and quieter, and it began to feel as if they were all alone in the big city. The night was hot but Olivia shivered. She was grateful that Georgia and Aeysha were with her. If she'd been on her own, she would have felt too frightened to continue, and without Alfie, who seemed to know every close and wynd of Edinburgh, they would have got hopelessly lost even with their map.

Even so, Olivia still wished Tom were here. They had been texting, but she had found it hard to explain everything that had been happening. The good news was that he'd soon be in Edinburgh. She couldn't wait to see him again.

A sudden yowl of a cat made them all jump, and Georgia gave a little scream.

"Sssh," hissed Olivia sharply, even though she felt as frightened as Georgia.

But Aeysha said calmly: "Livy, I hardly think your gran is going to pop out from behind a dustbin and announce that we're all excluded from the Swan."

Olivia grinned. "I wouldn't put it past her," she said, relaxing a bit. She knew that Aeysha was right. But she didn't want to get her friends into trouble. At first she hadn't wanted them to come with her at all and hadn't told anyone that Evie had told Jack that Mitch was responsible for the house swindle, and also where he could be found. Pablo, Michael and Jack were going to confront him tonight.

When Olivia had asked her dad why he didn't just go to the police, he'd looked sceptical and said that they would prefer to sort it out themselves. If the case went to court, it could be months before he got his money back, and he needed it now.

Evie had given him a good description of Mitch, and said he always left the same pub around the same time in the early hours of a Friday morning. Jack, Pablo and Michael would have surprise on their side. They'd be in a public place and Jack was certain they'd be quite safe. After all, there would be three of them. Besides, Jack said that Evie had become quite agitated when he'd mentioned the police.

I bet she did, thought Olivia to herself, but she didn't say it out loud in case he got all disapproving again. She just couldn't bring herself to trust Evie. So she said instead: "I want to come with you."

But Jack had shaken his head and said it was impossible. "I know you mean well, Liv, but you'd be more of a hindrance than a help, chick. I'd feel I had to look out for you as well as myself."

"But what if he gets violent?" asked Olivia anxiously.

"We're not going for a fight. It's the last thing we want. It's just to let him know that we know what he's done and where we can find him and that we will involve the police if he doesn't hand back the money. I hope it will be enough. At the very first sign of violence, Pablo and Michael and I will back off, I promise. We won't do anything silly."

Olivia hadn't been happy about it at all, but there was nothing she could do. Nothing, that is, until she found a torn scrap of paper in his room with the name of a pub, a street name and a time scrawled in his untidy handwriting. As soon as she saw it, Olivia knew what she was going to do: she was going to go to the appointed place, find a lookout spot and be ready to call for help if anything bad happened. Just in case. She decided to ask Alfie if he'd come with her, because his dad would be there, too, but Georgia and Aeysha soon got wind of the escapade because of the constant whispering and insisted on coming as well.

"Four is much safer than two," said Aeysha firmly. "One to get hurt, one to scream, one to run in circles like a headless chicken and one to summon help. At least that's what my mum always says."

"But if Gran finds out, we'll all get excluded. You heard what she said to Evie and Tati about running around Edinburgh in the middle of the night," said Olivia anxiously. "You'd be mad to risk getting chucked out of the Swan."

"Well, we'll just have to make sure we don't get caught," said Georgia. Olivia looked at Georgia and Aeysha's determined faces and thought how lucky she was to have such loyal friends.

In the still, dark night she was even more pleased to have them by her side. They had stuffed pillows in the four-poster bed the three of them were sharing just in case anyone checked up on them, and then they'd gone into Alfie's room, clambered out of the window and down the apple tree. It had felt like a great adventure at that point, but now Olivia was scared and she knew from the others' tense faces that they were, too.

She realised they hadn't come up with a plan of what they were going to do if things turned nasty. They turned another corner and came to a small unkempt square with a number of dark alleyways leading off it. In the corner of the square was a pub from which came the sound of shouting. The door suddenly opened and two drunken men were thrown out on to the street. One of them had a bloodied nose. The children shrank back into the shadows. The men stood up, swearing and cursing, and stumbled off into the night.

Alfie beckoned the others and they ran across the square to take refuge in the darkness of the stairwell of a tenement block. From there, they had a good view of the door of the pub. A dog barked nearby and they all jumped.

Olivia looked at her watch. Still at least fifteen minutes to go. Time passed slowly as the children huddled together, then Olivia thought she heard a noise and peered out. Was that somebody running soundlessly towards the flats that edged the alley opposite or was it only a shadow? She thought she caught movement on one of the walkways outside the flats, but maybe it was just a cat or a fox. Suddenly she heard a tiny noise on the other side of the square and Jack and Pablo appeared, padding as quietly and nimbly as cats. Michael brought up the rear, more flat-footed without their years of circus training.

For a terrible moment, Olivia thought that they were going to try to hide in the same place, but then, hugging the shadows, the men made their way around the square and disappeared into the darkness of another stairwell.

They all waited. Olivia squinted at her watch in the dark. It was almost 1.45 a.m. Maybe the man wasn't going to come. Maybe Evie had fed Jack misinformation. Another few minutes passed, and then the door of the pub swung open and someone came out. Olivia recognised him at once. It was the man who had been on the Mound on the first day she had seen Evie and Tati. The same man who had been in Greyfriars Kirkyard and lurking in the shadows on the Royal Mile. What was Evie and Tati's uncle doing here?

He started to walk away from the pub, his

phone in his hand. Jack and Pablo followed him, making almost no noise. They moved quickly behind him into the alley that ran between the walkways of two blocks of flats. Michael waited and then followed.

Olivia gasped when she heard her father speak. "Oi, Mitch," he said. "We haven't met, but you'll know me, and we need a little chat. It's about the money you owe me."

The man stopped. He swung round and smiled lazily. Olivia was horrified. Her dad had got completely the wrong man! This wasn't Mitch, this was Evie and Tati's uncle. Olivia was about to warn her dad, but just then, the man spoke.

"Oh yes," he said, with a nasty smile. "The great Jack Marvell, isn't it? It was like taking sweets from a kiddie."

Olivia felt shivery. She realised that she was the one who'd got it completely wrong. She felt such an idiot and she could see from Georgia's appalled face that her friend felt exactly the same. Ayesha had said that you shouldn't believe everything people told you and she'd been right. Olivia had been angry with Jack because he had been innocent enough to let himself be scammed, but Mitch had been taking her and Georgia for a couple of suckers, too.

"Look," said Jack. "I don't want any trouble, I just want my money back."

Mitch sneered. "And you thought if you asked me nicely, I'd just hand it over. You're all the same, you circus people. Think you're one big family. Hear you've even taken little Evie in." He saw Jack's surprised face. "Oh, I have my spies. It suited me to have her out the way. That kid's nothing but trouble. I suppose it was her who told you where to find me? Well, I wouldn't trust that one, if I were you. She'd sell her own grandmother. Double-cross her own sister if she felt like it." He paused. "Could be she's even led you into a trap."

He pressed a button on his phone, and from out of the shadows, six men appeared. Three stood behind him while three came up directly behind Jack, Pablo and Michael. Olivia recognised two as the men she and Georgia had seen coming out of St Giles' Cathedral.

Jack and Pablo looked behind them and realised that they were kettled in the narrow alleyway. Michael grimaced and looked wildly around. The men began to close in on them very slowly from either end of the alleyway.

"This is bad. We should call the police," whispered Aeysha, looking scared. Olivia didn't answer. The police would never get here in time. Jack and the others were going to get beaten to a pulp. She made a gesture that meant *stay there*, and ran out of the stairwell and across to the side of the alley without making the slightest sound.

She ran up some stairs directly in front of her. As she had supposed, they took her up on to the walkways that overhung either side of the alleyway. Bent double so she couldn't be seen, she crawled quietly along the walkway until she was almost directly above her dad, uncle and Pablo. Cautiously, she peered up over the wall and as she did so she thought she sensed somebody on the opposite walkway, but she didn't have time to worry about that now.

Down below, the scene was tense. The six men were still advancing. Mitch had stepped to one side. Pablo whispered something to Jack, who muttered something to Michael. Olivia's heart was beating very fast. Mitch must have known that the three of them were coming. They had been led into a trap by Evie!

Olivia was furious, and her anger made her bold. She took a deep breath and felt a bit sick. If she got this wrong, she could break both her legs. In one silent, seamless movement, Olivia hoisted herself on to the edge of the balcony and crouched there on the tiny ledge. The men below were so intent on each other that they didn't notice anything.

Three of the men had stopped a few metres from Jack and Pablo. Mitch nodded. One of them stepped forward, and took a swing at Jack, who jumped nimbly to one side. He took another swing and, as he did so, Olivia launched herself off the side of the ledge and right on top of the other two, who helpfully broke her fall by collapsing into a heap below her.

As she'd leapt, she'd been vaguely aware of a black-clad figure wearing a balaclava jumping from the balcony opposite. That figure took out two of the men approaching from the other end of the alley. They were now also lying on the ground, winded but not badly hurt. Some punches were being thrown by those men left standing but Mitch and his cronies no longer outnumbered the others, and Jack and Pablo were masters at avoiding their blows and much fitter and stronger.

From somewhere in the distance came the sound of a police siren. A dog began barking. Mitch and his bully boys looked at each other and scarpered. The shadowy figure melted into the darkness. Jack turned to his daughter in astonishment. "I don't know what you're doing here, and believe you me, I will expect a full explanation, but right now we have to get out of here." Jack grabbed Olivia's hand.

"Wait!" she said. "I've got to get the others."

"Others?" enquired Jack. "Don't tell me you brought the entire circus!"

"Not quite," said Olivia with a grin. "Just a few I can always rely on in a tight corner."

Chapter Twenty-Four

Jack was lying on the sofa in Michael's living room. He was holding a packet of frozen peas on his eye, trying to keep the swelling down. Michael had a cut on his forehead, while Pablo had some bruising on his arms.

"I reckon we'd have taken quite a beating if you hadn't turned up, Liv," said Jack.

"Yes," said Pablo mournfully. "Three grown men saved by a slip of a girl. I'll never live down the shame."

"It wasn't just me," said Olivia. "I couldn't have done it without Georgia, Aeysha and Alfie."

"I wasn't sure whether to call the police or not," said Aeysha awkwardly. "But I was so worried that the three of you were going to get really hurt."

"It was absolutely the right thing to do," said Jack reassuringly. "You weren't to know that Liv was going to do her crazy flying squirrel impression. It was brilliant thinking, Liv, brilliant and extremely dangerous. You'd better not do anything so reckless ever again. If you'd been just a few centimetres out, it could have been the end of your high-wire career, maybe even the end of you."

"I know, Dad," said Olivia. "But I didn't know what else to do. I thought those men were going to kill you."

"And I'm grateful, chick, but please don't ever leap off a balcony again," said Jack. "I'd hate to think what your grandmother's going to say about all this."

"Maybe she need never know?" said Michael innocently.

"The thing I want to know," said Alfie thoughtfully, "is who was the other jumper?"

"It all happened so fast, and it was all so chaotic and dark that I wasn't sure I could believe my eyes," said Georgia. "Whoever it was didn't stick about to leave a name."

"It's so weird that they had exactly the

same idea as me," said Olivia.

"The question is," said Aeysha, "was whoever it was there because they knew what was going to happen, or did they just happen to see what was going on and decide to pitch in?"

"OK, Aeysha, which do you think is more likely?" asked Georgia, sounding slightly scornful.

"Well, one thing is clear," said Jack. "Mitch knew we were coming and was completely prepared. He must've been tipped off."

"Who else knew you were going?" asked Aeysha.

"Clearly rather more people than I realised," said Jack drily. "Me, Pablo, Michael. You lot. Did any of you tell anybody else?" Everyone shook their heads solemnly.

"It can only have been Evie," said Olivia fiercely. "She must've betrayed you. I knew she couldn't be trusted. You should have listened to me, Dad."

Jack sighed. "It does look that way," he said. "But I trusted her…"

The door to the living room flew open and Tati stood there, white-faced. She had obviously been listening outside. "You're wrong," she cried. "It wasn't my sister. Evie would never do such a thing. It was me. It was me who told Mitch that you planned to surprise him."

"But why, why would you do that?" demanded Olivia angrily.

Tati's eyes flashed. "It's all right for you lot. It's easy for you. You're all so privileged, and you don't even know it."

"What are you talking about?" asked Olivia hotly. "None of us are privileged. We're just ordinary. My dad and Eel and I don't have any money. You know that."

"I'm not talking about money," said Tati scornfully. "Although it helps, money always helps. I'm talking about safety nets. Nobody is going to let you starve. You always know where your next meal is coming from and if you don't, somebody in your family will help you out and give you a roof over your heads. Like your gran did. You're all so rich and you don't even realise it. You're rich in family and friends.

"Evie and I have nobody. We walk the wire of life on our own. There is nobody and no safety nets to catch us if we fall. Evie and I have nobody, nobody except each other, and…and…" She burst into tears. "Soon we won't even have each other. Not if Mitch has his way. Evie will be put in a children's home or maybe even prison, and we'll be split up…"

Tati was sobbing so hard that she couldn't continue to speak. It was the longest speech that any of them had heard her make and they were all shocked and chastened by her obvious desperation. Olivia ran over and put an arm around her. Jack put his arm around Tati's other shoulder. Her body heaved but the sobs gradually subsided.

"Tati," said Jack gently. "Nobody's going to be angry with you, but I really think you need to explain what's going on."

Georgia handed Tati a box of tissues and the girl wiped her eyes. She looked round at all the expectant faces and took a deep breath. Just as she opened her mouth to speak, there was a furious barking and whining from the street outside.

"Harry!" said Tati, looking frightened. She bolted into the hall and opened the heavy front door. Harry leapt at her, barking wildly. He held her sleeve between his teeth and tugged at it as if trying to make him follow her.

"Harry! Where's Evie?" asked Tati

anxiously. "Why isn't she with you?" Harry whined again, and tugged urgently at her sleeve.

"Evie's in trouble," cried Tati. "We've got to find her!"

Chapter Twenty-Five

The Swans set off in the minibus towards the centre of town with Harry showing them the way from the front seat. Tati had wanted him to lead them on foot, but when they got outside the house, Harry had leaned with his paws against the bus and barked so loudly and insistently that a light had snapped on in the house opposite.

"Clever dog, he's telling us to take the bus," said Aeysha, astonished. So they had piled into the bus and Harry proved far better than any satnav. He sat next to Pablo, and when he wanted Pablo to turn he barked and if Pablo turned the wrong way, he growled and whined.

As they headed up through the New Town, Olivia suddenly said: "I know where he's taking us. Calton Hill!" She was right, and as the bus pulled up into the car park, they saw smoke. "Oh no!" cried Olivia.

The smoke was pouring from one of the dressing-room tents. Flames were licking at the canvas and shooting upwards as they were caught by the wind. Through the smoke they saw a desperate little figure trying to douse them with buckets of water from the standpipe in the car park. It was Evie, her face smeared with smuts from the fire.

"Help me!" she shouted when she saw them. "If it spreads, the big top will be lost too."

Everyone ran frantically to her aid. Pablo quickly set up a hose from the other standpipe.

"Call the fire brigade, Liv!" said Jack urgently.

"I've already done it," shouted Evie, and at that moment they heard the sound of sirens.

The fire engines arrived not a moment too soon. Another few minutes, and the big top would have gone up, but the firemen quickly brought the blaze under control, making sure it didn't spread beyond the dressing-room tent. An hour later, the firemen left, leaving everyone sitting in an exhausted heap on the grass as the sun began to rise over Edinburgh.

"Evie," said Jack, "I can't thank you enough for saving the circus. If the big top had caught fire, that would have been it for us."

"I don't think that's the only thing we've got to thank Evie for tonight," said Olivia quietly, picking up a balaclava she had found abandoned by the standpipe. "You were at the square earlier, weren't you? It was you who jumped over the balcony and helped save my dad and uncle and Pablo, wasn't it?"

Evie grinned a little shyly. "Great minds think alike," she said. "You and me, Livy, we make a great team. We worked together really well. I hope we can do the same on the high-wire. You're a great artist, Livy, and brave with it."

"Not as brave as you, Evie. Tonight you've been a real friend to the Swan Circus, and to me and my dad. To all of us, in fact," said Olivia. Then a thought struck her. "How come," she asked curiously, "you were here when the fire broke out?"

Evie shrugged. "I've been sleeping here most nights since my name appeared in that review," she said. "Tati has, too, sometimes. This is where we were on the night of the storm. I know the way Mitch's twisted mind works and was certain that once he'd connected me with the Swan Circus, he'd find a way to get at all of us. He'd already tried to trick Tati and me into meeting him at St Giles' Cathedral but we gave him and his heavies the slip."

Evie paused to take a breath. "I knew that he'd be particularly furious about what happened tonight and that he'd take his revenge, so I came straight here and waited. I thought Mitch would just trash the place, but about half an hour after I got here he turned up with a can of petrol. Fortunately he was a bit drunk and he didn't do a good enough job."

"The firemen said they thought it was arson," breathed Aeysha. "They're sending somebody to investigate in the morning. He could go to prison for this."

"I wish," said Tati softly.

Evie looked hard at her sister. "I suppose it was you who told Mitch that Jack knew where to find him?"

"I had to," said Tati desperately. "He ambushed me on the Royal Mile and told me that if we betrayed him, he'd run you over and break your legs. He knew that we were with the Swans. He's clearly been keeping an eye on us for some time and waiting for his chance. Moving in for the kill."

"I knew he was getting serious when he drove that car at us," said Evie. "I knew it was a warning. I'm sorry you got hurt in the process, Livy. But after that review, I knew he'd know for certain where we were and I realised we were putting you all in real danger."

"Mitch says that he's finished with Edinburgh and he's leaving soon," said Tati. "I think he's in trouble with some of his former cronies. Before he leaves he wants the sapphires and if you don't hand them over, he said you're going to regret it for the rest of your life. Actually what he said was that, 'She'll regret it for the rest of her life – if she has a rest of a life.' Oh, Evie, I was so scared that I thought if I told him what Jack had planned, he might leave us alone."

Tati started weeping again. Evie hugged her. Georgia was looking at them with a puzzled expression. "I'm very confused," she said. "Is this Mitch person also your uncle?"

Evie and Tati shook their heads fiercely. "That's what he calls himself, but he's not a real uncle. We haven't got any family in this country."

"I think," said Jack, "that you'd better tell us the whole story right from the beginning."

Chapter Twenty-Six

"By the time we arrived in Edinburgh, Mum was desperate," said Tati, settling into the sofa back at the house. "She knew she didn't have long to live, and she knew that if she died that Evie could be taken into care and we'd be split up." She bit her lip. "It was one of the reasons she said to tell everybody I'm eighteen. I won't actually turn eighteen for another few months. Aunt Rhona seemed a better bet than a children's home. She was our insurance policy against the future."

"But Aunt Rhona had died by the time you got here, hadn't she?" said Aeysha, remembering the conversation around the campfire on the first night Evie and Tati had come to the campsite.

"That's right," said Evie. "But there was

one good bit of news. Aunt Rhona hadn't much money but she'd left Mum the only things she had of any value: a sapphire necklace and some earrings. They weren't worth a lot, but the few thousand pounds would make all the difference to us. We thought that if Mum improved we might even be able to rent a little flat for a few months."

"That's the necklace that Alfie filched from your pocket during his magic act, isn't it?" said Georgia excitedly.

Evie produced the necklace with a flourish. The sapphires caught the light and sparkled, and everyone oohed and aahed over them.

"So it *is* real," said Georgia.

"That's why you were so upset about Alfie taking it," said Olivia softly.

Evie winced and nodded. "I'm sorry, I know I was rude but I was upset."

Olivia looked hard at Evie. If she was lying, she was a very good actress. Olivia suddenly felt relieved that all her fears about Evie seemed unfounded, although there were a great many questions that still needed answering. Like why Evie had all those newspaper cuttings in her box.

"So," said Olivia, the words slipping out before she had really thought them through. "The necklace really does belong to you after all."

Evie looked surprised and affronted. "Of course it does. What did you think we are: jewel thieves?"

Olivia blushed bright red. Everyone turned to look at her. She wished she'd kept her mouth shut. Everyone was waiting for her to explain what she'd meant.

When Olivia didn't say anything, Evie raised her voice. "You did, didn't you?" she cried. "You thought we were thieves!"

"No, no, I didn't," protested Olivia, unable to meet Evie's eye. She wanted to fall through the floor. "It was only that, I found these..." She reached into her pocket and pulled out the cuttings about the jewel thefts.

Evie stared at them, her face white. Her eyes were burning and she said very quietly. "It's OK, Olivia, we all know that you can't resist nosing into everything and then jumping to all the wrong conclusions."

"Hold on, Evie," said Aeysha very calmly. "I believe that the necklace really belongs to you and isn't stolen and I'm sure that Livy does, too. She's not making any accusations, she's just asking some questions. You and Tati *have* been very secretive, and you haven't always told the truth. Maybe it's not surprising that Livy is asking questions?"

Evie looked furious. Tati put her hand on her sister's arm. "Evie, Aeysha's right. We owe them an explanation."

"I saved their circus for them, didn't I?" said Evie mutinously. "I shouldn't have to prove myself to anyone."

"You did save the circus, Evie," said Tati gently, "but if it wasn't for us, the Swan Circus wouldn't have been at risk in the first place." She looked around at the Swans and the grown-ups. "You've all been so kind to us and we've brought you nothing but trouble. I'm sorry."

Jack went to speak but Evie cut him off. "Not that I owe you an explanation, Olivia, especially as you shouldn't have been going through my stuff in the first place, but the reason I saved the cuttings was because I was trying to gather evidence that linked Mitch to the hotel robberies." She flipped open her phone, and showed them the series of shots of Mitch in various hotels around the city.

"Tati and I followed him as much as we dared to and snapped him whenever we could when we saw him going into one of the big hotels. We thought he was probably staking them out, because the hotel would always be robbed a day or two after his visit. We kept them as proof of the connection between Mitch's visit and a subsequent robbery."

"But why didn't you just go to the police and tell them your suspicions?" asked Alicia gravely, who had heard them return to the house and had slipped into the room and listened hard as Evie and Tati told their story.

Evie and Tati looked flustered. "We rang in an anonymous tip-off from the campsite phone box, and the police stopped the robbery but Mitch got away."

"I still don't understand why you didn't go to the police in person, they'd have listened to you," said Alicia.

Something suddenly occurred to Olivia. "Has he got some kind of hold over you?" she asked.

Tati and Evie looked at each other. "Come on, Evie," said Tati eventually, "we need to come clean and tell them everything."

Evie gave a heavy sigh and then she began: "We met Mitch at the hospital the day after Aunt Rhona's solicitor had turned up with the sapphires and earrings and all the papers for Mum to sign. At the time, Mitch turning up seemed like a complete coincidence, but now I'm not so sure that it was."

She shook her head, and then continued. "The meeting with the solicitor took place in the corner of the ward day room. It wasn't very private, but there wasn't anywhere else to go. There were other people in the room, most of them patients watching TV, but there were some visitors, too.

"We tried to get as far away from everyone as we could but there was a man sitting quite close with his face hidden by a newspaper. Looking back, I think that must have been Mitch. He'd have overheard everything – the solicitor checking that Mum really was Cora Purcarete, formerly Cora McDonald, of 13 Jekyll Street and Flat 4a, Horriston Terrace, Morningside, and saw him handing over the sapphires and earrings to Tati. I think he was just in the right place at the right time and seized the opportunity."

"The solicitor had wanted us to leave the jewellery with him for safe-keeping, but Mum said we should turn it into cash. We had the documents to prove they were ours, so why not? She knew she didn't have long," said Tati sadly.

"For the rest of the day I had the strangest feeling that we were being watched, but I didn't really think anything of it. We made an appointment with a jeweller's for a valuation the following afternoon, but when we went to visit Mum the next morning, Mitch was there by her bedside. He said it was a happy coincidence; he'd been visiting a relative in the same ward and he'd recognised Mum: they'd worked together in the same circus in Spain before we were born.

"Mum was dopey from all the drugs she was taking, but she seemed to confirm that she knew him, so we took all his smiles and offers of help at face value. He seemed really interested in the fact that I could walk the high-wire. He even charmed the nurses and he told them that he was our uncle. Mum took a turn for the worse before lunch, so we never made it to the jeweller's, and when she died later that evening we were so distraught we just let Mitch bundle us up and take us back to his flat."

"It was a mistake," said Tati grimly. "The first of many. In the morning, the sapphires and earrings were gone, and Mitch turned out to be far less charming than he appeared. He kicked Harry and shut him out of the flat. We were virtual prisoners. It was clear he was involved in a great many scams and that he was also a jewel thief. He was using his old circus skills to scale buildings and run across roofs, but he was out of condition and it was getting too dangerous for him. He thought he'd found the person who could do his dirty work for him. Evie."

Evie looked at Olivia, her eyes burning. "So yes, Olivia, you're right. I *am* a jewel thief. Or rather, a failed one."

"Mitch promised that if Evie did just one job for him, then he would hand back the necklace and earrings," continued Tati. "She refused, of course, but Mitch said that without the sapphires, Mum would be given a pauper's funeral in an unmarked grave. We were desperate and grief stricken, and we believed him."

"What happened?" asked Aeysha.

"I climbed up on to the roof of the hotel and in through the window of the room he'd told me to. The diamond earrings Mitch wanted were lying on the dressing table in the empty suite. It would have been so easy to take them. But I just couldn't." Evie looked close to tears. "It felt so wrong. So I didn't. I just left and told Mitch that I'd been disturbed and had to leave in a hurry. Which was true, really, because as I climbed out of the window somebody came into the room and saw me. Fortunately I was wearing the balaclava. It was a narrow escape."

"Mitch was furious, and angrier still when Evie demanded the sapphires and said that if he didn't hand them over, we'd go to the police," said Tati. "So that's when he played his trump card."

"What was that?" asked Eel, wide-eyed.

"He said that my fingerprints would be all over the hotel room and window ledge and that if we sneaked to the police, I'd be the one in trouble. He'd already found out that Tati wasn't eighteen after all and said that the authorities would split us up and put me in a children's home. He said I might even be put in prison. We were really scared. We didn't have any adults we could turn to."

"I wanted to run away," said Tati, "but

Evie wouldn't leave without the sapphires. She said Mum wouldn't have wanted us to. So we watched and waited. Tried to pretend to Mitch that we were beaten, and that Evie would do the next job he wanted when it came up. We started to gather evidence of what he was up to. We knew about the house scam and that he was using 13 Jekyll Street as the address. One night, when he was drunk, he accidentally left the key to his safe where we could filch it. As soon as he was asleep and snoring we opened the safe, took the sapphires and fled. Only we dropped the earrings as we left the flat and Mitch woke up, so we had to leave them."

"Is that when you moved into the garage?" asked Olivia.

"Yes," said Evie, "We'd been on a little pilgrimage with Mum to see where she had lived as a child when we'd first arrived in Edinburgh, so we knew about the garages. I'd noticed that the padlock on one of them was broken. It felt like a place where we could feel close to Mum, and although he was using the address for the scam, we knew Mitch had never been there."

"Weren't you scared he'd come looking for you?" asked Georgia.

"It was way off his patch," said Evie. "And in many ways he's quite stupid. We reckoned the safest place to hide out was in the most obvious place. Often you don't see what's right under your nose.

"But we were getting worried that he might find us, and then he caught us lurking near one of the hotels where he'd been, and after that he began trailing us across the city. We had a couple of close calls, but Harry saved us," said Evie, hugging the dog, who licked her face. "We didn't know anywhere else to go."

"I wanted to leave Edinburgh," said Tati. "But Evie wouldn't hear of it. She said she wasn't leaving until we had the earrings, too. Evie is very determined."

"We've noticed." Alicia smiled.

Evie blushed. "But then you lot turned up in town. We only came to the circus and the workshop because somebody gave us a flyer for free tickets. It was better than being in the garage, and well out of Mitch's way. He was becoming very persistent. I was surprised to see you, Olivia, and I'm afraid I was still angry with you about the magic show, so I booed you. Then at the workshop I walked the high-wire and Jack offered us a role in the show. It seemed like the answer to our prayers. I thought it could give us a breathing space and some protection until we worked out what to do next."

"We were horrified when we discovered that Jack had been the victim of one of Mitch's scams," said Tati.

"We never meant to cause you trouble," said Evie quietly.

The grown-ups looked at each other. "We believe you, of course we do. The question is, what are we going to do about you now?" Jack looked worried.

"We'll sort something out," said Alicia. "It's the least we can do. You've been through a great deal, girls, but you're safe now. It's time to go to the police, get this mess cleared up and make sure Mitch gets everything he deserves."

Evie looked as if she was going to cry. "But if we go to the police, the social services will become involved and I could end up being sent to a children's home, couldn't I? Tati and I want to stay together."

Jack looked agonised. "Alicia, we can't guarantee that won't happen, can we?"

Alicia shook her head.

"Please, Miss Swan, please wait. Just give us a couple more days. You'll be leaving Edinburgh soon anyway, and I want to get Jack's money back for him before you go. I know how I can do it, and it's the least Tati and I can do after all the trouble we've caused. A few days won't make any difference, surely, and it would mean so much to us," said Evie.

She looked so desperate that Alicia relented, even though she shook her head and said she wasn't sure she was doing the right thing. But it had made both Evie and Tati beam.

Chapter Twenty-Seven

Olivia sat down on the grass next to Evie feeling shy. Evie grinned at her. Olivia didn't think that Evie and Tati had much to grin about, and after hearing their story, she didn't feel much like smiling either. She felt guilty. Really guilty.

"Evie, I'm so sorry," she whispered. "I really didn't mean to accuse you of being a thief."

Evie just smiled more. "I know that, Olivia. And I should never have booed you. It was wrong and arrogant of me. Livy, I am a very good tightrope walker; you will be a great one."

Olivia smiled. "Well, you're going to be the world's best dog trainer," she said.

"Yes," said Evie, sounding very like Eel. "I am." She grinned at Olivia.

"Evie," said Olivia. "How exactly do you plan to get Dad's money back for him?"

"Oh," said Evie. "That's easy. I'm going to make Mitch an offer he won't be able to refuse."

"What?" asked Olivia, puzzled.

"I'm going to offer to swap the sapphires for the money he swindled from Jack. They're worth much more to him. Particularly as he's got the earrings, too."

Olivia was appalled. "But you can't do that! The necklace is the only security that you and Tati have. You can't give it up just so Jack gets his money back. Jack won't let you. *I* won't let you."

"Ah," said Evie with a little secret smile, "but I don't see how you can stop me."

The roar of the crowd subsided, the Swans took their last bow and ran out of the ring. It had been an electrifying performance, with everybody on top form. Alfie's magic act had been much appreciated by the crowd, and Olivia and Evie's high-wire duel was so charged that the audience gasped and then cheered. The fairies and the animal procession had been utterly enchanting, and when Jack and Olivia had done their high-wire act it had felt as if the whole tent was holding its breath. It was just as well. A five-star review in the *Guardian* that morning as well as the growing word of mouth had ensured a full house, and two people had been in from the team that awarded the prestigious Fringe Firsts, including the chief critic of the *Scotsman*, a dark-haired woman who had beamed and clapped wildly when Alfie had stolen her notepad and biro without her noticing.

It was beginning to look as if the Swan Circus might triumph after all. On the strength of it, Alicia had decided to splash out on getting some proper glossy programmes printed and they were selling like hot cakes. Olivia and the others were still pumped full of adrenalin but rather than running back into the dressing-room tent, they ran a little way down Calton Hill and sat on the grass together.

"You do realise that if Gran catches us still in our costumes, we'll all be toast," said Eel warningly.

Olivia ignored her. "So," she said, looking at the others very seriously. "Have you had a chance to think about my plan. Are we agreed? We'll put the plan to Evie and Tati and if they think it's a good idea, we'll put it into action?" Everyone nodded.

"But will it work?" said Aeysha, looking anxious. "The trouble is that we won't know until we do it," said Georgia. "It's risky, but it's worth a try."

"But after everything they've been through, we've got to do something to help Evie and Tati," said Olivia. "After all, she's trying to get Dad's money back. I'd feel so guilty if I just let her do it without trying to help in some way. Tati was right, compared with them we've all got it made."

"You musn't feel guilty, Livy, that you were suspicious of them. If I'd known about the newspaper cuttings, seen the photos and overheard the same conversations, I'd probably have thought so too," said Aeysha.

"Alfie," said Olivia, "are you certain that you're up for this? So much depends on you. We can't do it without you."

"Oh, he's been practising like mad," said Eel confidently. "He even managed to make Harry disappear this morning."

"Well, all of him except his bark," laughed Alfie, "which rather gave the game away."

"Fortunately," said Aeysha, "humans don't bark much." Then she added thoughtfully, "Although, of course, Evie does have a bit of a bite."

They all laughed before hurrying away to take off their costumes before Alicia caught them. Olivia went to find Evie and Tati. If they agreed to try Olivia's plan, the Swan Circus was going to have to give the performance of its life.

Chapter Twenty-Eight

Evie slipped down the aisle to where Mitch was sitting in the second row. Olivia had directed him to that seat after she'd torn his ticket when he came in. Evie sat down in the empty aisle seat next to him. He had a small suitcase tucked between his feet.

The show was almost halfway through, and out of the corner of her eye, Evie could see that Alfie was getting ready to do his next solo conjuring act that would take them up to the interval. In the ring, the Swans were doing their sequence on the silks and Kasha's dreamy music was helping to create a genuine sense of enchantment. In their sequined costumes and sleek green and aquamarine leotards with leggings, their faces covered with streaks of blue and green make-up and touches of glitter, the Swans looked like exquisite, ethereal creatures from another dimension. Everyone was lost in the performance and didn't notice that the thickset man and the girl in the second row were behaving slightly oddly.

"Have you got the money?" hissed Evie, out of the corner of her mouth. Mitch kept his eyes on the show in the ring but nodded.

"Show it to me," said Evie.

"Oh, Evie, don't you trust your uncle Mitch?" said Mitch with a sly grin, his eyes still fixed on the performance.

"You're not my uncle and I have no reason to trust you," snapped Evie.

Mitch opened his programme and inside Evie could see a wad of notes. She eyed them carefully and got him to fan them out. She wouldn't put it past him to put a few real £50 notes on the top and then plain paper cut to size underneath.

"Where's the necklace?" demanded Mitch in a loud whisper. Evie indicated the programme that was on her lap, and opened it so that he could see the jewels. Mitch's eyes gleamed and he ran his tongue over his lips greedily.

"You do realise," he said silkily, "that I'm only doing this out of the goodness of my heart. I'm giving you much more than the necklace is worth."

Evie snorted. "Come on, Mitch, everyone knows you haven't *got* a heart. You were in the wrong queue when they were handing them out. You're giving me the money because you know that the necklace is worth three times the money you swindled out of Jack, and because you know it's your last chance to get it before you leave Edinburgh for good. I've been making a few enquiries and you're getting out because there are a lot of people in this city who are very upset with you and all your double-crossing."

"You know nothing," sneered Mitch. "Let's just get on with it and I'll be on my way. The Costa Brava here I come."

"I think," said Evie softly, "that you better look behind you." Mitch turned round. A sheen of sweat appeared on his brow. A few rows further up in seats on either side of the aisle were two burly men he clearly recognised and wasn't at all pleased to see.

"You wee double-crosser. You've lured me into a trap," he snarled. "The deal's off."

"I had no idea they'd be here," said Evie. "But tell you what, I'll help you get away. It suits both of us. Let's do the swap, and then you just stay put until the next act. It's a conjuror. He's very good, even though he's only a kid. When he asks for a volunteer from the audience, you get down there smartish. We'll conjure you out of the big top so you don't have to come face to face with your two friends up there."

Mitch looked around wildly. He could see that he was trapped, and had no choice but to go along with Evie's plan.

"All right," he said gruffly and he pushed the programme towards her. She took it carefully before handing hers over. The silks sequence was coming to an end. Evie ran nimbly up the steps, taking great care of her bulky programme that she had shoved under her hoodie out of sight of prying eyes. She ran out of the big top and round to the performers' entrance, where she found Olivia waiting for her with Alfie and Tati.

"Slight change to Olivia's brilliant idea," she announced as she handed Olivia the programme with the money and pulled off the jeans and hoodie that she was wearing over her leotard. "Alfie, you not going to make Tati and me disappear as Olivia suggested, you're going to make *Mitch* disappear. It couldn't have worked out better if we'd planned it," She continued to swiftly explain what she wanted him to do.

Will, in his elephant costume, was just concluding squirting the audience with water and the music was changing. This was the cue for Alfie to take to the floor with his disappearing act. The audience had already enjoyed Alfie's act with the rabbits and they were looking forward to seeing what he did next. Olivia ran around to the back of the band. Kasha saw her coming and just raised himself very slightly from his seat, allowing Olivia to secrete the bulging programme underneath him. It would be quite safe there until the interval. He winked at her and played on.

Out in the ring, Alfie was wearing his too-big-for-him hat and the cloak with its crescent moons. He was busy charming the audience with his patter.

"And now, ladies and gentlemen, boys and girls, I'm going to make a member of the audience disappear. But I'm going to need all your help. I can't do it on my own. This is such a stupendous undertaking that I simply don't have the power alone. I need all your magical powers to help me to magick a volunteer into another dimension."

He waved his wand with a flourish and opened the front and back doors of his box. It looked like an exotic wardrobe, covered with tiny silver stars and magic squiggles. The audience could see daylight on either side.

"Now," said Alfie, "I need a volunteer. It must be an adult and it must be someone strong and brave who is prepared to travel through time and space."

The drama in his voice made the audience smile but nobody had their hands up.

"Come on, ladies and gentlemen," said Alfie, wagging his finger at them as if they were all naughty children. "There must be someone here with a spirit of adventure, someone strong and brave who is not easily frightened, who is in a hurry to get somewhere…"

Mitch had his arm up and was waving it around in the air.

"Sir," said Alfie, walking towards him and putting out his hand to draw him into the ring. "Let me congratulate you on your courage. I always think that it's really important to have witnesses when you're about to do something really brave, and you, sir, have an entire audience to clap and cheer you on your way."

Mitch looked suspicious as if he thought that he was being made fun of but couldn't quite work out how it was happening. There was something comical about the way the small boy was leading the sweaty man clutching his suitcase. The two burly men jeered.

"I'm glad to see that you came prepared for a long journey, sir," said Alfie with a grin.

Evie and Olivia looked at each other. "I think your cousin might be slightly overdoing it," said Evie. "I wish he'd get on with it. We don't want Mitch turning nasty. He's got a horrid temper."

Alfie opened the door to the box with a flourish and ushered Mitch in. It was a tight squeeze.

"Are you sure that you're quite comfortable, sir?" said Alfie, giving Mitch a good pat as if he was a dog. "You look a little hot, sir, let me cool you down," and he waved his arms around Mitch in a fanning motion. Mitch had gone very red in the face. "Now, sir, are you quite sure that you are ready for your journey?"

"Yes," snapped Mitch. "Get on with it."

"Gran," said Olivia to Alicia, who was standing with them, watching. "You know you were very keen to call the police and tell them about Mitch? I think now might be the moment to do it."

Alicia looked at Evie, who nodded. "Yes," she said with great satisfaction. "Livy is right. It's the perfect moment. Tell them to come to the bottom of Calton Hill if they want to catch the jewel thief."

With a lot of arm-waving, Alfie made a great show of locking the box. Then he pulled across a small sliding window in the top of the box through which Mitch's grimacing face could be clearly seen. He looked so uncomfortable and so clearly not brave that the audience laughed. This made Mitch furious, which made them laugh all the more. Alfie hurriedly pulled the sliding window shut.

"Right then, ladies and gentlemen, boys and girls, we're going to do some magic. Remember, I can't do this without you. I need you all to think very hard about a tropical island, and through the power of thought alone we will transport this brave man to an island paradise. So all together now, think hard while I wave my magic wand."

Kasha and the band struck up, the music sounding like a spell. Alfie waved his magic wand. He muttered an incantation. He tapped the box once, twice, three times, and then with a flourish he pulled back the window. There was no sign of Mitch.

"He's sat down," cried out a child in the audience. "He's still in the box, hiding."

"Oh no he isn't," said Alfie with a grin, playing to the crowd.

"Oh yes he is!" they chorused delightedly.

"Oh no he isn't," said Alfie, undoing the locks and throwing open the doors of the box. It was quite empty. There was a moment of astonished silence and then the crowd erupted with a roar, and began to clap wildly. The two men who had been tailing Mitch looked at each other, shrugged as if neither of them could quite understand what had happened to Mitch, and made hurriedly for the exit.

Mitch was halfway down Calton Hill. He couldn't believe his luck. That little Evie had actually done him a favour and helped him out of a tight spot. All he had to do now was take the sapphires and the other stolen jewels he had in his case to a fence who would give him a good price, and then he would head straight to Edinburgh airport and get himself out of the country. Soon he'd be far away on a permanent sun-soaked holiday. Silly kid, those sapphires were worth far, far more than the sum he had swindled out of that sucker Jack Marvell.

Mitch patted his inside jacket pocket where he had secreted the sapphires for safe-keeping. A wave of nausea swept over him and he almost stumbled. The necklace wasn't there! Or the earrings. He felt in all his other pockets, but he knew that he wouldn't find them. They had been filched by that boy-magician. He was certain of it. He gave a howl of rage and turned around, determined to go back to the circus and raise merry hell. He'd kill that Evie Purcarete who thought she could get one over him.

He broke into a run, and as he did so, he saw the two men he most didn't want to meet in the world coming towards him. He turned on his heel and fled, but as he reached the main road he heard a police car screech to a halt and saw two policemen leap out and run towards him. Two more police cars arrived.

Mitch dropped his precious suitcase and it fell open. A ruby brooch tumbled on to the pavement. One of the policemen scooped the brooch and the suitcase up, and the other lunged for Mitch and brought him down. Mitch struggled as his hands were forced behind his back and into handcuffs. He knew that he wouldn't be heading off into the sun after all. He groaned and rued the day he had met Evie Pucarete or heard of the Swan Circus.

Chapter Twenty-Nine

"It's so exciting!" said Aeysha, looking out of their dressing-room tent at the long queue snaking from the box office. "It's going to be another full house."

"We're completely sold out tonight, too. Returns only," said Eel happily.

"We deserve to be full," said Evie. "The reviews have all been raves. Look, Livy, there's a massive picture of you and Jack on the high-wire in the *Guardian*. They say 'this is a truly enchanting show that will make every child – and adult – want to run away and join the circus.'"

The Swans were all buzzing with excitement. They'd just come from the ceremony at which they had been awarded their Fringe

First, and there was a strong rumour that they were going to get a Herald Angel, too. A TV crew was going to be filming part of this afternoon's performance, and producers from both the Barbican and the South Bank were coming to see the show with an eye to transferring it to London the following summer. Both Alicia and Jack had told them not to get their hopes up.

"Producers are fickle," warned Alicia. "They get all excited about a show but it only lasts five minutes and then they move on to what they think will be the next big thing." She looked thoughtful. "In any case, if we did want to bring it to London perhaps we should produce it ourselves?"

Jack looked horrified. "I never want to produce anything again in my life," he said. "It's much too stressful. I'd prefer to spend forty days and forty nights living on a high-wire than go through the agonies of doing all that again."

"That might be wise, Jack," said Alicia drily. "Not forty days and forty nights on the high-wire. That would be insanity. But no more producing. You should stick to the creative and technical stuff and leave me to do the rest." She smiled at her son-in-law. "Together we could make a great team."

"We already do," said Jack quietly.

There was a cough outside the girls' dressing-room tent, and a familiar voice said: "Is everyone decent? Can I come in?"

Georgia, Aeysha and Eel squealed, and Olivia flung back the tent flap and threw herself on the freckle-faced, red-haired boy standing outside.

"Tom McCavity, where have you been all summer?" she cried.

Tom laughed, "Flying to Neverland, since you ask, but I'm back in the real world now and dying to see your show."

"See it! Now you're finally here, you're going to be in it. We've still got ten performances to go," said Olivia. "We'll have you rehearsing first thing in the morning. Dad will be thrilled."

"I'm a bit rusty," said Tom.

"Oh, the high-wire's like riding a bicycle," said Olivia. "You never forget." Ayesha went to greet her family, who'd travelled up to Edinburgh with Tom. Georgia went to look out for her dad and Leonie, who'd also come up on the same train to stay for a few days.

Olivia introduced Tom to Evie and Tati.

"These are my great friends, Tom: Evie and Tati Purcarete. Evie and Tati are an essential part of the Swan Circus, and part of the Swan family." Evie and Tati went pink and looked really chuffed. She also introduced Tom to Alfie.

"My cousin," she said proudly. Tom was impressed by Alfie's conjuring prowess, and Alfie was even more deeply impressed to discover that Tom could walk the high-wire.

"It's almost the end of the summer. Term will be starting soon," said Aeysha when she came back to the dressing tent. "I can't believe that we'll be going into Year Nine."

The Swans started talking about school, the people they knew and how much they were looking forward to the coming term. Everyone was talking so animatedly that nobody really noticed Evie and Tati detach themselves from the group. Nobody except Olivia, who followed them around the back of the dressing room.

"Why did you leave?" she asked.

Evie blushed. "Whatever you say, Livy," she said, "Tati and I, we're not really Swans."

"Yes, you are. You're honorary Swans. Just like Alfie."

"But after this summer, we may never see

each other again," said Evie, wistfully. "Alicia is talking to the social services. They're trying to work something out."

"You know that Gran would have you at the Swan, Evie. If that's what you wanted."

"What do you think I am," said Evie, looking comically affronted. "Some kind of stage-school brat?"

Olivia laughed. "That's what I thought about all stage-school kids before I went to the Swan. But I was wrong. Most of them aren't like that at all."

"No," said Tati. "They're not. They're loyal and brave like you, Livy. You are lucky to have such good friends."

"I know," said Olivia seriously. "We all look out for each other."

"Ready to catch each other if you fall," said Evie softly.

"Yes," said Olivia. "We all need people like that in our lives. There's somebody out there for you and Tati, Evie. I'm sure of it. But in the meantime, you'll just have to make do with me and the Swans. We're good catchers, honest."

"The best." Evie smiled.

* * *

It was after the evening performance. The sun had almost set but it was still blisteringly warm. It was so still that from across the city they could hear the sound of the Tattoo coming from the castle. Soon there would be fireworks. The Swans were celebrating the end of a blissful day with a post-show picnic on the hill. Michael and Lydia had made masses of salads and quiches and there was a huge raspberry cheesecake and two chocolate cakes for pudding.

Olivia and Tom were sitting together on the hillside.

"This is magic," said Tom, stretching out. "You are lucky to have spent the entire summer here."

Olivia smiled to herself. If only Tom knew. It was going to take a long time to tell him everything that had happened, about all the misunderstandings there had been and all the mistakes she had made.

"Tom," she said haltingly, "you know the way that sometimes you think that you are on the right track…"

"…but it turns out that you are on completely the wrong train," said Tom, finishing her sentence for her. "Been there, done that."

He squeezed her hand. Olivia smiled into the dusk. She'd always known that Tom would understand.

She looked across the hillside. Alfie was trying to teach Eel how to produce an egg from behind Emmy's left ear; Jack and Michael were laughing together; Aeysha was surrounded by her large family; Georgia had her arm around her mum's waist as they both stood chatting to Georgia's dad and Leonie. They all looked relaxed and happy. Olivia heard Georgia say: "Can I? Can I really?" The adults all smiled and nodded, and Georgia put her hand on Leonie's swelling tummy. A look of wonder came over her face.

"I felt her. I felt my baby sister kick!" she said excitedly. "I can't wait until she's born and I can hold her and help look after her."

"Families are such funny things, aren't they?" said Olivia.

"Yes," said Tom. "Sometimes I want to kill mine, but I wouldn't be without them."

"Me neither," said Olivia.

"I'll remind you that you said that the next time you're raging at Jack or in a strop with your gran or irritated by Eel."

Olivia watched a chic dark-haired woman walking up the hill. She was peering anxiously around as if looking for somebody. Her eye suddenly fell on Evie and Tati, who were talking intently to Alicia. The woman's worried face broke into a broad beam as she called out their names and started speaking very fast in a foreign language.

Evie and Tati looked up, astonishment passed across their faces, then they ran towards her and threw themselves into her arms. Harry barked as if in welcome. There was a great deal of gesticulating, Tati burst into tears, and Evie was talking at high speed in what Olivia guessed was Romanian and grinning from ear to ear.

Evie turned to the others. "I would like to introduce you to our Auntie Zsa Zsa."

"Are you quite sure she's your auntie?" asked Eel, very seriously. "Because your uncle wasn't your uncle."

"Certain," said Evie, with a grin.

"Yes," said Zsa Zsa in almost perfect English. "Evie and Tati are my dead brother's children. Poor little orphans. I had no idea that poor Cora had died, too. I've been trying to trace them for months, and then I had a stroke

295

of luck. I was doing yet another online search and Evie's name came up in a review of a circus production at the Edinburgh Festival. I caught the first plane I could and I've come straight here from the airport. I can't believe I've found you. I thought you were lost to me for ever. Now we can all be together again. A real family." She burst into noisy tears.

Evie looked worried. "Are we going to have to move to Romania, Auntie Zsa Zsa?"

"Oh no, Evie, darling. I've been living in Italy working with a circus as an animal trainer. But my contract is almost up. I'll be a free agent by Christmas. I can live anywhere in Europe. Even Edinburgh, if that's where you want to live. I have a little nest egg that will see us through, and I'm sure I'll find work. I noticed some very badly behaved dogs on my way from the airport in the taxi. These poor people and their doggy friends, they desperately need our help, Evie. It's our duty to lend a hand."

Harry bounded up and offered his paw. Zsa Zsa smiled. "You trained him, Evie?"

Evie nodded.

"I knew it," said Zsa Zsa happily. "You've remembered everything I taught you. We'll make a great team!"

"And what about Tati?" asked Alicia softly.

"Oh, I'll be fine," said Tati, with a big grin. "If I know that Evie's going to be looked after, I can go back to college, get some exams and maybe go to university." She looked shy. "I'd like to be a doctor. Maybe I could find a cure for leukaemia."

"That's all quite settled, then," said Zsa Zsa decisively, with the confident air of a woman who knows that life is really very simple and that there is no need to complicate it. "Now let's celebrate and then you must tell me everything that's happened to you."

As Kasha and the band started to play, fireworks began to explode above the castle, fizzing across the sky and streaking it red and silver and electric blue. Georgia was dancing with her dad; Aeysha was gambolling with two of her little sisters; Lydia and Michael were dancing; Alfie and Eel were hamming it up with Tom; and most astonishingly, Jack and Alicia were dancing a gentle waltz together in perfect step and time. It was, thought Olivia, a magical scene.

Evie detached herself from Tati and Zsa

Zsa and came over to Olivia.

"May I?" she said, giving her a mock bow.

"Enchanted," said Olivia, bowing back, and the two of them joined in the dance. They whirled into the middle of the dancers. Evie's foot grazed the side of a tussock and she stumbled, but Olivia didn't falter. She gripped Evie firmly and she stayed upright. The two girls smiled at each other, swaying and spinning together in perfect unison, ready to catch each other if they fell.

About the Author

Lyn Gardner was born in London and now lives near Richmond Park with her partner and two daughters. A theatre critic on the *Guardian*, she goes to the theatre five or six nights a week, which should leave no time for writing books at all. But apart from the **Olivia** books, she has also managed to write two other novels for children: *Into the Woods* and *Out of the Woods*. Her ambitions are to learn to tap dance and walk the high-wire, but it may have to be the low-wire as she is a bit scared of heights.